THE GREEN REICH

Drieu Godefridi

ISBN 978-2-930650-24-1

To environmentalists of all parties.

Table of contents

Introduction – "Never Again"

I grew up in a time when the phrase "never again" still had resonance, its subject the atrocities of the Second World War. Never again, in this context, meant not repeating the horrors of National Socialism and a World War in which, judged by the sheer number of victims, was the worst butchery the world had ever seen.

"Never again," *Nie Wieder Krieg*,[1] had been much voiced after the First World War. Yet, only two decades later came further abomination, even worse than its predecessor.

"Never again" means nothing if one confines oneself to contemplating and deploring the past. This formula makes sense only if the idealist's trope is transformed into an analytic proposition exploitable here and now, that is to say, applied to the ideologies of the present time. Otherwise, the words "never again" are meaningless.

This reworking is all the more desirable as history teaches us that the great totalitarian systems, their ideologies, and even their leaders, kept no secret of the atrocities they intended to commit.

As early as 1920, Adolf Hitler demonstrated, in a founding speech in Munich, his execration of the possessive Jew, instituted in the antithesis of the egalitarian and racial socialism that he claimed to favor. The post-1945 choruses of "we did not know," of the extermination of the Jews by the National Socialists, seemed somewhat questionable considering that the entire National-Socialist theoretical corpus tended towards demanded and legitimized in advance, and, *ab initio*, the extermination of the Jews.

---

1 "Never again war."

Hate is no less present in the writings of Marx. The fervid denouncing of the bourgeois, the veritable eulogy of violence that is not only a means of revolution, but a technique of government, is the substance of Marxist political theory. Violence and arbitrariness are not merely a necessary evil during the transitional phase (the seizure of power) but conferred as the legitimate and primary tools of government. Such as these figured prominently in the writings of Marx and his cohorts—including the extolling of civil war and concept of *Volksrache*—decades before the first communist regime took shape.

"Never again." When esteemed environmentalist thinkers demand the abolition of democracy and freedom "for the climate"; when these thinkers earnestly purport to demonstrate that the good of the Earth requires the reduction of the population to one-tenth of its current volume; when there takes shape, before our very eyes, an ideology more radical in its homicidal intent than any of its predecessors; it is then that we must once more take up the cry of "never again" and understand that hard times are, indeed, again upon us.

7th of October 2019

7th of October 2049

"Principle 1. Gaia is alive"

(*Vade Mecum for the Common Man*, 2022)

— *Dad, I still have that toothache. Will you take me to the dentist?*

— *Matthew, you know that your monthly CO_2 ration is used up. Look … it is the 7th. More than 24 days to wait. I will make an appointment.*

— *Dad, when you were little, could you go to the dentist as often as you wanted?*

— *Well the dentist has never been my favorite destination; but yes, you're right, in the Old World, we went to the dentist as often as we needed.*

— *And did you have to walk for hours like nowadays?*

— *My mother took me there by car.*

(Silence). Then, Matthew:

— *What a terrible time you lived in … All that pollution. At least we are rid of that!*

— *The pollution was atrocious, it made us gag.*

— Before the school was closed, we were shown images of the cities back then ... the darkness, those stained facades, the "smog" as in the London of Dickens or that of Sherlock Holmes. Everything so black, so dirty!

The father smiling:

— I'm not that old. You're talking about the end of the nineteenth century!

After a moment's hesitation, Matthew, with all the surety of his 12 years of life experience:

— Dad, in the photos with mom, why are the facades not black? It was well before the Great Stop!

— I do not know. The facades of the monuments were often renovated using horrible chemicals, which consumed incredible amounts of fossil energy!

— You know, Dad, three days ago, in your library, I found a little book by a certain Gerondeau. I did not understand everything ... but he explains that the pollution in Paris in 2018, so 4 years before the Great Stop, had already been reduced to almost nothing ...

— How absurd! I shouldn't keep those Fossil Era authors, and you shouldn't read them.

— But ...

— The problem, you see, Matthew, was CO_2. We produced insane volumes. CO_2, as the Official Program has taught you, made our beautiful Earth uninhabitable. Sophia-Gaia was violated by Man!

— Yes, Dad, I know. I know all that.

The father, getting carried away:

— Yes, you know it, because you've been taught it! But you can't imagine the reality of these monstrous globalized companies who were constantly disemboweling the Earth to steal resources and then quickly squandering them; the oil rigs that drilled into Our Mother, Man's infernal workings without rhyme or reason to enrich what we called "shareholders" ... Man was guilty of attempted Terracide!

After a moment's silence:

— Dad, when you were my age, how many people were there in our country?

— 60 million.

— And now?

— There are 25 million, I think ... too many! Thank goodness we have the Official Altruistic Death Program. It is poetic that hangers-on from the fossil era, instead of persisting in their misuse of resources, choose to be humusated. Then their non-being returns to the true Being. A toast to your mother's memory!

— In our village, I am the last child.

— Evidently.

— So, soon, nobody will be left!

— Only the Nomenklatura of the Resources, which will ensure the regeneration of Sophia-Gaia in the millennium to come. In their last report, before accomplishing their mission and

subsequent dissolution, the IPCC scientists considered the possibility of environmental regeneration by man's absence for several centuries...

— *Centuries!*

— *What are a few centuries against the millennia of depredation of Sophia-Gaia! Poor creature. (The father meditates for a few moments on the perversity of Man.)*

Matthew, resuming:

— *Do you remember Isabelle, the last girl in my class? She said that before the Great Stop, people got married, started families, had children, raised them and took them on ... I forgot the word...*

— *Holidays! To defile the planet at home was not enough for them; it was necessary for them to despoil everywhere, as Hans Jonas said!²*

— *Isabelle said that people liked to have a holiday from polluting at home.*

— *Oh yes, of course, left to his own devices, the Accursed Parasite would despoil the entire Universe! Blessed be Sophia-Gaia that this girl left the region.*

— *You know, dad, there is something weird. If Isabelle did leave the region, as you say – how did she do it? There isn't any transport anymore! ... And, she would have said goodbye...*

---

2 "Man despoils Nature in the most ruthless fashion:" Hans Jonas, interview with *Der Spiegel*, 1992, https://www.spiegel.de/spiegel/print/d-13680535.html

— *Oh yes? And why would she tell you? You know it's a CO_2Crime to commit an LPJ (long pointless journey)?*

— *I know that, dad! But ... (hesitating) Listen, we were only small, but we talked to each other ... Isabelle told me that her dream was to start a family ... with me!*

— *CO_2Crime!*

— *CO_2Crime, OK. But I thought she would have told me she was going. And then, there was her mother, seriously ill, waiting for her Humusation Order. How could she have moved?!*

— *Frankly, I do not know.*

— *What if the Nomenklatura took them?*

— *Why would they do that?*

— *For CO_2Crime! For committing acts that uselessly produce CO_2! Maybe for having a child, the CO_2Crime par excellence!*

The father is thoughtful. Then:

— *What if they did? Do you want to return to my time, that of the hubristic Parasite that disemboweled Mother Earth? The Nomenklatura is, and will be, in centuries to come, the benevolent martinet in all matters, for as long as the Fallow Period lasts. We have no choice but to put our trust in them. We must have faith in them.*

Matthew's turn to be silent.

— *Dad, what will be my future? What will I do in ten, twenty, or thirty years?*

— Thirty years?! Do you want to be a geriatric? (The father laughs.)

— What will I become?

— Don't think of your individual self! I will not always be able to protect you against CO_2Criminal impulses! Be careful, you do seem prone to those impulses.

— What will I do with my life?

— What we all do now: embrace the rhythm of the seasons and the light of the True Day, waiting to return to Her nurturing womb. Our lives—yours, mine, that of your late mother—only make sense through, and in connection, with Our Earth. We ... we, execrable individuals ... we are nothing. The nobility of our position resides in the consciousness of being only modest reflections of the living totality.

FIRST PART – ENVIRONMENTALIST THEORY

First, we will try to highlight the theoretical elements common to the different currents of environmentalism as a political ideology. Let's start by tackling the misunderstanding that reduces environmentalism to a simple novation of Marxism.

I.   Environmentalism is not Marxist

The material overabundance of modern technology
is an essential factor in the modern socialist ideal.

Hans Jonas, *The Principle of Responsibility*[3]

In one particular essay on socialist civilization,[4] the passion for equality—in the sense of real, material equality—is presented as the seminal principle of socialism in its various theoretical accretions and practical applications.

The passion for equality is not foreign to environmentalism. The majority of practical environmental proposals could well appear on the agenda of a Marxist or radical socialist party such as today's Democrat Party in the United States.

The struggle against inequality is constantly presented by environmentalists as a necessary step towards the reconciliation of Man and the Earth.[5]

3 Paris, Flammarion, 2013 (1970), 275.

4 D. Godefridi, *La passion de l'égalité — Essai sur la civilisation socialiste*, 2017.

5 See the latest IPCC Special Report, SR15, Summary for Decision Makers, 20 and the report proper, chapter 5, especially page 479.

The rejection of the capitalist production system, or market economy, is another common point. Long before the birth of the theory of anthropogenic global warming (AGW), environmentalism rejected capitalism in principle and the full gamut of its applications.

Consumerism was denounced in connection with the exhaustion of resources. Is capitalist exploitation of resources tolerable? Is the inheritance by future generations of a world in some way stripped, reduced and exhausted, acceptable?

We will have recognized the theme of development, which is acceptable only if it is *sustainable*, a theory which prevailed prior to the theory of the AGW;[6] yet, today, most contemporary ecologists reject the very idea of "development."[7]

Despite these convergences between socialism and environmentalism—egalitarianism and the rejection of capitalism—their fundamental differences are obvious.

Even though it may seem paradoxical, Marxism, the ideology that caused the death of one hundred million people in the twentieth century,[8] is nonetheless, in principle, humanistic. According to Marxism, Man is the measure of everything. Man, and beyond that, Mankind, because Marxism is universal, transcending race,

6 The first international conference on the role of carbon dioxide and other greenhouse gases in climate change was held in Villach, Austria, in 1985, under the auspices of the United Nations Environment Program (UNEP) and the World Meteorological Organization (WMO).

7 Fabrice Flipo, "The Three Concepts of Sustainable Development," *Sustainable Development & Territories*, Vol. 5, no. 3, December 2014, section 5 "Exiting Development," references cited.

8 S. Courtois et al., *Le livre noir du communisme*, Paris, Laffont, 1997, p.14.

ethnicity, history, and nation. Man is the *ultima ratio*[9] of Marxism. There is no Marxist historical structure except in and by man; nature is virtually absent from the Marxian theoretical corpus.

Marxism is productivist and promises abundance. It does not reject industrialization *per se* but proposes that the State seizes the means of economic production. It aspires to *dognat i peregnat*, as Stalin said, to catch up with and overtake the production of capitalist societies. This has never been achieved by Marxist society but it does not negate its theoretical framework. In short, Marxism dreamt, naught but a dream denied by its praxis,[10] of establishing equality through abundance. Hans Jonas makes the exact same point: "In the case of Marxism, the magic of a great utopian vision of a fairer society coincided with a promise of happiness, namely that increased control of Nature would benefit everyone, equally."[11]

This productivism is foreign to environmentalism; it is even antithetical to it.[12] Environmentalism does not intend to seize the means of production to increase and distribute the fruits in an equal manner. Environmentalism plans to seize the means of production to stop it.

---

9 i.e. the ultimate rationale.

10 i.e. the practical implementation.

11 "Im Falle des Marxismus traf der Zauber einer großen, utopischen Vision einer gerechteren Gesellschaft zusammen mit einem Glücksversprechen, daß nämlich die weitere Meisterung der Natur nun allen zugute kommen wird, und zwar gleichermaßen," interview with *Der Spiegel*, 1992, https://www.spiegel.de/spiegel/print/d-13680535.html.

See, also, his interview with *Esprit* by Greisch and Gillen, "From Gnosis to Responsibility Principle," May 1991, No. 171, p.18: "The joyous Marxist utopia has forged a strong alliance with science-based technology." https://esprit.presse.fr/article/jonas-hans/de-la-gnose-au-principe-responsabilite-entretien-11883

12 "Though the enemies' of environmentalist society' are inarguably on the side of the forces of capitalism, it would be wrong and dangerous to forget that they are also part of the history of the Left and, for the most part, of socialism": Serge Audier, *La société écologique et ses ennemis*, Paris, Seuil, 2017.

It is not the ownership of the means of production that is in question; it is the very existence of the said means. If Marxism promised abundance, environmentalism promises only destitution, uncertainty, decay, and, finally, *chosen* misery.

II. Early Environmentalism

Man is, everywhere, a disturbing agent.
Wherever he plants his foot, the harmonies
of Nature are turned to discords.

George Perkins Marsh (1864)[13]

The perpetuation of our economic
system is physically impossible.

William Stanley Jevons (1865)[14]

Environmentalism is a doctrine endowed with political pretensions; this predates the theory of anthropogenic global warming.
The first signs were found during the nineteenth century, in the
works of Henry David Thoreau (1817–1862) and Elisha Reclus
(1830–1905); in 1864, George Marsh published *Man and Nature*,
denouncing the depletion of resources, the disfigurement of the
countryside by Man, and already "the harmful role of private cor-
porations." In 1866, the term *ecology* was coined by the German
zoologist Ernst Haeckel.

13 *Man and Nature: Or, Physical Geography as Modified by Human Action*, New York,
C. Scribner, p.36.

14 *An Inquiry Concerning the Progress of the Nation, and the Probable Exhaustion of
Our Coal Mines*, MacMillan (1865).

The dominant thesis of that nineteenth-century proto-environmentalism was that, by his savage, indiscriminate, and unlimited exploitation of resources, ineluctably, Man exhausted them. This early environmentalism was Malthusian, named after the British economist, Thomas Malthus who, at the turn of the nineteenth century, formulated a thesis of the collapse of humanity as a result of its exponential increase relative to a mediocre linear increase of resources.

In the twentieth century, the works of authors such as Arne Næss, Ludwig Klages, Aldo Leopold, Hans Jonas, and Dave Foreman built the first specific theoretical structure of environmentalism, pleading terrestrial ethics, the recognition of the 'human' rights of animals and the ecosystem, the halting of progress, and the renunciation of technology.

According to this un-anthropocentric ethical framework, Man is but one creature amongst others. The prodigal primate re-joins nature, often designated since 1970 under the name of the goddess Gaia (à la James Lovelock), personifying the Earth as being alive.[15]

This ontological degradation of Man is a key aspect of contemporary environmentalism.

15 *Gaia: A New Look at Life on Earth* (OUP, 1979).

III.   A "Physisist" Ethic, or Relapse

The environment is a living whole.

Etopia[16]

From the Greek *physis* meaning Nature; the *physisist*—non-humanist— ethics of environmentalism mark a radical break from western tradition.

In all its components, egalitarian and materialistic socialism measures all things in the light of the material reality of Man.

Just as anthropocentric is the ethic of liberalism, economic and technological progressivism. This ethic champions man, his freedom, and his personal enterprises in the broadest sense of the term.

Christian ethics are strictly anthropocentric, despite St. Francis of Assisi's celebrations of Nature, never deified, and the environmental concessions of the recent strange papal encyclical *Laudato si'*. In Christian theology, Man alone was created in the image of God. Nature is in no way disregarded, but is only the crucible of the creature made in the image of God: Man.

The American ecologist Lynn White was not mistaken when he repudiated Christian anthropology in *Science* in 1967: "Hence, we shall continue to have a worsening ecologic crisis until we

16 Center for training and research in political ecology, associated with the Belgian party "Ecolo."

reject the Christian axiom that Nature has no reason for existence other than to serve Man. (...) Both our present science and our present technology are so imbued with orthodox Christian arrogance toward Nature that no solution for our ecologic crisis can be expected from them alone. Since the roots of our trouble are so largely religious, the remedy must also be essentially religious."[17]

To round up this brief overview of the backdrop of tradition, let us mention Heideggerian phenomenology, which places Man in unique transcendence, consciousness and as the source of meaning. Three "monopolies" that make the *Anthropos* the axis of Heidegger's rational world.[18]

It is possible by stepping away from tradition to encounter other ethical *physisists*, because ethical physisism is not an environmentalist invention.

Take, for example, the Gnostics, of whom we know all too little, but enough to understand the basis of their relationship with the world. A formidable melange of Greek, Semitic, Roman, and Christian influences, Gnosticism, which flourished in the second century, sees in Man the reflection of a pure and perfect God, imprisoned in his bodily condition by a bad and evil God.

Man's intrinsic knowledge is directly entrusted to him by the pure and perfect God. Corporeality is perceived by the Gnostics as a confinement, a bond, a mere pause before the return to the perfect God. The domestication of Nature, *the very Nature of our*

---

17 10 March 1967, volume 155, no. 3767.

18 Martin Heidegger, *Etre et Temps (Being and Time)*, Paris, Gallimard, 1986 (1927), p.36: "The Dasein is a being who does not appear only among other beings, what distinguishes him ontically is that, in his being, he goes for that being *of* this being (...) What ontically distinguishes Dasein is that it *is* ontological. "

existence on this earthly plane, are considered anomalies; salvation can arise only from abstention from the world, while awaiting the return—by death—to Purity.[19]

It is useless to engage in any misguided attempt to establish a genealogical link between environmentalist ethics and Gnostic ethics. As far as we know, there is no author, school, or environmentalist chapel that claims any link with the Gnostics.[20]

How can one not recognize the similarity of their ethical philosophy?

How can we not see that the abstention from worldly matters of Gnostics cannot be distinguished from the abstention requisite by environmentalists? How can one not see the similar disqualification—by differing means—of Man's mastery of Nature?

If the environmentalist ethic is distinguished from the Gnostic, it is by its radicality:[21] the Gnostics recognized, in Man, a providential link to the divine, with even human knowledge stemming

---

19 Here are the characteristics of the Gnostic ethic according to Yves Chalas, *Vichy et l'imaginaire totalitaire:* salvific knowledge of totality, Manichaeism involving a heroic fight against the advocates of evil in this world, redemptive affliction as an intermediate phase between the initial fall and the fulfilment to come (Actes Sud, 1985, p.46).

20 Hans Jonas worked on Gnosis and Gnostics. His doctoral dissertation (under Heidegger's direction) is entitled *Der Begriff des Gnosis* (1928, I thank Professor Ernest Mund for bringing this to my attention). He also published the very detailed *Gnostic Religion* (1958) although he could not take into account the discovery of the texts of the Egyptian Gnostics at Nag Hammadi. If Jonas considered that Gnosticism informs our vision of Nature and Man, he did not expressly include "environmental ethics" – but in fact, a metaphysic of Nature - in direct filiation of Gnostic ethics (see below).

21 If Jonas refuses to inscribe his environmental ethic in direct filiation of the Gnostic ethic, it is because Gnosticism seems to him too "dualistic," giving Man a specificity - an insularity - that nothing, according to him, can justify. In this sense, Jonah's ethic is more radical - in his ontological degradation of Man - than Gnosticism ever was (*La religion gnostique*, Flammarion, 1992, p.440). See also his interview with *Esprit*, May 1991, p.9.

from the divine. There is no such thing in environmentalist ethics,[22] which recognizes no primacy of Man of any kind except in his ability to harm the "All Living."

In Genesis, Man is driven out of the Garden of Eden but still retains his transcendence. According to environmentalist ethics, Man suffers further degradation, being driven out of his transcendence.[23]

The environmentalist ethic is *physisist* and even physico-morphist because it recognizes, in most of its declensions, the living reality of the ecosystem: "the environment is an ecosystem, that is to say *a living totality organized by itself (spontaneously)*"[24], explains Etopia, the center for training and research in political ecology associated with the Belgian party Ecolo (in a fourfold pleonastic formula)[25].

In all terminological rigor, there is no environmentalist ethic, only what Hans Jonas calls a "metaphysic of Nature."[26]

22 The imputation of pantheism - deification of Nature - which is made to environmentalism is arguable, but not necessary. The Environmentalist values Nature at Man's expense; such can be achieved by the ontological degradation of man, without the need to divinize Nature per se. The concept of "All Living" is pantheistic. See the attempt to understand the All Living, below.

23 Taking into account the transcendence of man, which is an objective reality, is what led the influential environmentalist James Lovelock to distance himself from Environmentalism itself: "We are the intelligent elite among animal life on Earth and whatever our mistakes, <Earth> needs us. This may seem an odd statement after all that I have said about the way 20th century humans became almost a planetary disease organism. But it has taken <Earth> 2.5 billion years to evolve an animal that can think and communicate its thoughts. If we become extinct, she has little chance of evolving another." *The Vanishing Face of Gaia: A Final Warning*, Basic Books, 2009.

24 https://etopia.be/introduction-a-la-philosophie-economique-et-politique-de-lecologie/

25 https://etopia.be/pourquoi-etopia/

26 Interview with *Esprit*, 1991, p.16.

Pestilent mammal, creature among creatures, the eco-human undergoes an ontological degradation unprecedented in western tradition.

In Search of Isabelle

"Sterilize! Sterilize! Sterilize!"

New Gospel According to Paul, 2024

Refusing to be satisfied with the convoluted explanations of his father, Matthew resolves to go in search of Isabelle and her family. The smokescreen of the "Big All" and other big this-and-thats with which they stuffed his ears before the school was closed now seemed useless. At the time of school, yes, of course, because the spoon-feeding of information about Man, his crimes, and our duties towards Sophia-Gaia, our mother, was incessant. The workshops on the concept of CO_2Crime in its many variations were also unforgettable! But all this was long ago, and Matthew now has another priority: finding his missing friend.

Matthew heads in the direction of the cottage that Isabelle and her family occupied, but soon hesitates. He knows that he won't find anything more than he did during his last visit, that is to say apart from Isabelle and her parents' personal effects (of course she had no brothers and sisters). For this reason, Matthew knows that his father is mistaken, and that Isabelle's family did not leave of their own free will. She must have been chased off or forcibly removed.

Matthew sets out again, this time towards the Nomenklatura of Resources complex, its nocturnal illuminations dimmed now that homes are no longer supplied with electricity between 10 pm and 7 am, an infernal glow.

IV.   The Population Bomb (1968)

*Hundreds of millions of people will
starve in the 1970s and 1980s.*

Paul Ehrlich, *The Population Bomb*, 1968.

In 1968, Paul Ehrlich demonstrated in *The Population Bomb* that human proliferation was leading to ruin and that a turning point condemning us to insecurity, famine, and ultimately, extinction, was imminent. There is to the discordance, as alleged by Malthus, between the arithmetic progression of resources and the geometric (exponential) progression of humanity, an appeal that has never been denied.

Ehrlich's work is based on classic Malthusianism: We now know that it is impossible to increase the production of food at a rate such that is in line with the growth of the population, says Ehrlich, advocating a wave of practical measures to curb the "cancer" of population: abortion, a radical means of population control, the introduction of sterilization chemicals into drinking water, a complete reversal of our value system, the change in our way of life, public re-education, and the forced sterilization by vasectomy of entire populations. Hindus and Pakistanis are expressly mentioned[27] as they have a regrettable tendency to reproduce "like rabbits." Ehrlich echoes the literal and assumed racism of Thomas Malthus.

Ehrlich's apocalyptic predictions— massive famines coming after 1980; hundreds of millions of people starving in the 1970s–1980s ; in 1984 we will be simply dying of thirst ; our teenagers today are unlikely to ever reach adulthood — all proved to be grotesquely false.[28]

Yet, *The Population Bomb* is, in many ways, a precursor. We can still find that unbridled anti-humanism in contemporary environmentalism, the will to reduce the human population to a fraction of what it is (Ehrlich speaks of 500 million), a drastic reduction that would be the final solution to the ecological problem and even the idea of instituting an International Tax for Survival, payable by over-developed countries to underdeveloped countries, the greater part being paid through the United Nations, because men and nations have learned how dependent we all are on each other and dependent on the health of our small spacecraft called Earth.

---

27 "When he [Indian Minister Chandrasekhar] suggested sterilizing all Indian males with three or more children, we should have applied pressure on the Indian government to go ahead with the plan. We should have volunteered logistic support in the form of helicopters, vehicles, and surgical instruments. We should have sent doctors to aid in the program by setting up centers for training para-medical personnel to do vasectomies. Coercion? Perhaps, but coercion in a good cause. I am sometimes astounded at the attitudes of Americans who are horrified at the prospect of our government insisting on population control as the price of food aid. All too often the very same people are fully in support of applying military force against those who disagree with our form of government or our foreign policy. We must be relentless in pushing for population control around the world."

28 Paul Ehrlich's literary career is marked by outrageous and absurd predictions—e.g. "I would take money that England will not exist in the year 2000"—that do not merit reproduction here; any interested parties wishing to kill time should google "Paul Ehrlich quotes."

These suggestions, which date back to 1968, prefigure the "Green Fund" institutionalized by the Paris Agreement (2015), which brings in the *annual* transfer, under the aegis of the United Nations, of $100 billion from the west to the rest of the world.[29]

Half a century after the publication of this book, the world population has never been so large; at the same time, famine has never been so rare. Technological progress—especially modern agricultural techniques and the so-called green revolution[30]—can better feed our current population than was possible in pre-modern times even though we only numbered a few hundred million.[31]

It will not have escaped anyone's attention that Mr Ehrlich's *Bomb* is based on a paradox of demanding a drastic reduction of the world's population to avoid a drastic reduction in the world's population.

29 "The Paris Agreement on Climate Change," https://www.consilium.europa.eu/fr/policies/climate-change/timeline/

30 Note that the term "green revolution" was coined by the World Bank to describe the miracles of agricultural progress in India and Pakistan, precisely the two countries for which the author of *The Population Bomb* prescribed vasectomy, forced sterilization and the introduction of sterilizing substances into the drinking water. Regarding the green revolution, see the remarkable synthesis of Guy Sorman, *The New Wealth of Nations*, Hoover Press publication, 1990.

31 The data published by the UN Food and Agriculture Organization (FAO) leave no doubt. 37% of the world's population suffered from malnutrition in 1970, compared to 12% in 2010. The announcements of recent years are complicated by the desire to promote the AGW theory. Thus, the article of the World Health Organization (WHO) - also under the auspices of the UN - September 2018 "Hunger in the World Continues to Increase": "821 million people are now suffering from hunger" (https://www.who.int/fr/news-room/detail/11-09-2018-global-hunger-continues-to-rise---new-un-report -says). Anyone who reads this text will conclude that indeed hunger in the world is worsening. However, compared to the global population, the percentage of people suffering from hunger worldwide has been less than 11% for four years (since 2014), a record in the history of humanity. This is despite a population that in some parts of the world continues to grow. The percentage of people suffering from hunger has never been so low in the history of humanity at the same time that humanity has never been so numerous.

V.　The Meadows Report (Club of Rome), 1972

There will be a desperate land shortage before the year 2000 if per capita land requirements and population growth rates remain as they are today.

Meadows Report, p.51, 1972

In 1972, the Club of Rome published the *Meadows Report*,[32] which is worthy of our close consideration. Not for its naive method, nor for its predictions since being systematically discredited, but for its foreshadowing of the contemporary environmental movement, including the IPCC reports.

Through the utilization of a limited number of factors—resources, available food per capita, world population, industrial production per capita and pollution—the authors of the Meadows Report propose simulations of possible outcomes from 2000 to 2100.

What all the "Meadows" simulations have in common is a prediction of the collapse of production and population if the aforementioned factors are left to develop of their accord. The only variable is the time—more or less imminent—of collapse. Figure 36 (p.127) predicts a "collapse" later than Figure 35— assuming larger than estimated reserves in 1970—but a collapse nevertheless: "The larger industrial plant releases pollution at such a rate (...) that the environmental pollution absorption mechanisms

32 Meadows, Meadows, Randers and Behrens, *The Limits to Growth*, 1972.

become saturated. Pollution rises very rapidly, causing an immediate increase in the death rate and a decline in food production. At the end of the run, resources are severely depleted in spite of the double amount initially available."

The crux of the argument lies in the limited Nature of "our Earth" and its resources (p.86).

To the Meadows Report's merit, it does take up the technology argument. The nuclear technology is accounted for, in its favorable effect on the exploitation of resources and on recycling (Figure 37). But alas, pollution will soon overcome these advances: inevitable collapse. The authors go so far as to imagine that nuclear energy will make it possible to control pollution better (Figure 39), but again, all in vain, because "These changes allow population and industry to grow until the limit of arable land is reached. Food per capita declines, and industrial growth is also slowed as capital is diverted to food production" (p.136); the collapse is, this time, due to the scarcity of food, because the limits of available arable land have been reached… Should we impose birth control? Collapse is postponed by only a decade "or two." It is quite the ruthless mathematical model.

The mistake of the proponents of technology is not to accept or understand the idea of the Limit: "The hopes of the technological optimists center on the ability of technology to remove or extend the limits to growth of population and capital. We have shown that, in the world model, the application of technology to apparent problems of resource depletion or pollution or food shortage *has no impact on the essential problem, which is exponential growth in a finite and complex system*" (p.145, italics added).

The Report goes on to accuse the "green revolution," although it acknowledges its merits, of possibly *increasing* malnutrition, because the poor cannot afford to buy the food produced (p.147). This is nonsense that is best overlooked.

What is the solution? Instead of denying the Limit, it is necessary to learn to live with it (p.150). The model then finds its equilibrium simply by stopping economic growth (defined as industrial production per capita) and controlling births in the most rigorous way.[33] Global Equilibrium will take place (Figure 46).

"Such counter pressures will probably not be entirely pleasant," the authors concede. For example, Americans will have to accept a modest reduction in their standard of living, in the order of 50% (p.165). A simple formality: either strike equilibrium or face collapse.

Of course, even in global equilibrium, resources will continue to dwindle, according to the definition of the resource concept by the reporters. However, do note the formula on page 166 that refutes all 165 previous pages: "Resources are still being gradually depleted {during global equilibrium}, as they must be under any realistic assumption, but the rate of depletion is so slow that *there is time for technology and industry to adjust to changes in resource availability.*"

The authors of the report refuse to say *how* the transition from growth to equilibrium will take place, nor how said equilibrium will be maintained; they do not seem to understand that if growth is halted, technological progress is halted, the two being consubstantial.

The Meadows Report, which is the village idiot of reason, is characterized by both its imagination and its formidable political posterity.

---

33 To prevent economic growth from collapsing, the Meadows Report recommends reducing it to zero.

This is the general tone of early environmentalism: essentially moral, although marred by scientizing claims on the Malthusian theme of the exhaustion of resources.

VI.   The Intellectual Vulnerability of Early Environmentalism

The ultimate resource is the human imagination coupled to the human spirit.

Julian Simon, *The Ultimate Resource* (1981)

Let us note the intellectual vulnerability of this early environmentalism. The erroneous variable is that of resources: through his technical inventiveness, Man exponentially increases the resources that can be exploited. As the philosopher Corentin de Salle has shown, in line with the work of the American economist Henry George (1839–1897) and especially of the economist statistician Julian Simon (*The Ultimate Resource*, 1983), even the very concept of "resource" is not, in fact, strictly natural.

It is thanks to his ability to exploit them that Man literally invented so-called "natural" resources, as we speak in law of the invention of a treasure trove.[34] The argument "yes, but the Earth is still limited" does not do justice to the precisely exponential and demiurgic nature of this invention of resources.

34 "Invention d'un trésor" in French, which means the discovery of something that was there but not "existent" before the discovery, e.g. old golden coins in a field.

Again, this whole debate is distorted by the obsession with fossil fuels. In which case, the distinction must be highlighted between *reserves*—i.e. proven resources—and *theoretical resources*, which are not located, or are located but are not exploitable. By definition, reserves are only a fraction of the resources.[35]

However, the resources of an economy are not limited to so-called raw materials. Let us go to the other end of the economic chain and look at the chicken population. When Man lived by hunting and gathering, the chicken population numbered less than one hundred thousand on the surface of the Earth. Today it is in the billions. The reserve/resource conceptual couple cannot account for the capacity of Man to *create* resources.[36]

What is important is not the existence of an overall theoretical limit—which no one disputes, and which is a truism, i.e., the principles of thermodynamics—but the exponential growth of exploitable resources, including primary materials, which prevents the theoretical limit from being ascertained, depriving it of *any* relevance, both in practice and in theory.[37]

The main resource of humanity is Man.

35 I thank Prof. Samuel Furfari for drawing my attention to the importance of this conceptual couple.

36 "An increase in the population of falcons leads to a fall in the population of chickens, but an increase in the human population leads to an increase in the chicken population," Henry George noted, quoted by Corentin de Salle, "L'archaïque conception cosmologique du WWF" (*The Archaic Cosmological Design of the WWF*), Itinera Institute, https://www.itinerainstitute.org/fr/article/larchaique-conception-cosmologique-du-wwf/

37 Which is incidentally recognized when the authors of the Meadows Report write: "There is no single variable called technology' in the world model. *We have not found it possible to aggregate and generalize the dynamic implications of technological development because different technologies arise from and influence quite different sectors of the model.*" (p.130, italics added)

VII.   The Empirical Vulnerability of Early Environmentalism

*Never in the history of humanity has Man
had to backtrack in his progress because
a raw material has failed him.*

Samuel Furfari, *Ecology in Wonderland*[38]

The last fifty years of Earth's history have witnessed the development of two concomitant phenomena: the population explosion and the decline in widespread hunger.

For the first time in its multi-millennial history, China has eradicated famine; at the same time, its population has never been larger. The same applies to India, Pakistan, and a number of smaller countries.

The few famines we still endure are usually caused by war, often in *under*populated countries such as Bolivia.

Taking the aforementioned Paul Ehrlich literally, in 1980, the economist Julian Simon proposed that he should choose five raw materials, not controlled by the government, and to set his own deadline to judge the evolution of their cost. In the Malthusian and catastrophic logic of Ehrlich, the price of these raw materials could only explode. Julian Simon, however, predicted that their price would drop. Ten years later, the price of the five raw materials

---

38 Paris, François Bourin, 2012, p.118.

chosen by Ehrlich had, without exception, dropped, even though the world's population had increased—between 1980 and 1990—by 800 million.[39]

Malthusianism is a theory that has never been verified in the history of any country. It has also been effectively refuted, theoretically and empirically.

However, ideology is invincible.[40]

39 Ed Regis, "The Doomslayer", Wired, https://www.wired.com/1997/02/the-doomslayer-2/ Ehrlich pursued a career in literary gloom-mongering.

40 One of the Meadows, Dennis, 40 years after the publication of the Report, stuck by his guns: "The common idea is, even today, that there are no limits. And when you demonstrate that there are, the general response is that it doesn't matter, because you're going to get close to that limit in an orderly and quiet way and you're going to have a soft stop because of the laws of the market. What we demonstrated in 1972, and which remains valid forty years later, is that this is not possible: crossing the physical limits of the system leads to a collapse." https://www.lemonde.fr/planete/article/2012/05/25/la-croissance-mondiale-va-s-arreter_1707352_3244.html

The Nomenklatura of Resources

"To die = to love"

Simplified Principles of the Nomenklatura of Resources, 2026

Matthew does not recall the precise moment of the coup by the Nomenklatura of Resources (NoR). His father explained to him that the NoR was established when, having reached maturity, humanity understood that its mission was to repair the planet to transmit it in a viable form to future generations. The NoR maintains branches or feelers throughout Europe and elsewhere in the world. Its hold on power allows for the rational management of resources in contrast to what his father calls the "fecal production" of capitalism. The past grows ever dimmer, however, since the voluntary disconnection of the internet network.

Matthew stands on the outskirts of the first perimeter of the NoR: simple electrified fences. This is as close as he has ever been. The NoR stretches as far as the eye can see. A huge, sparkling white complex enjoying the distinguishing feature of permanent electrification.

It is August and it is roasting hot in the full glare of the sun. Damn the anthropogenic global warming! thinks Matthew. Selfish bastards from previous generations, scavengers of the All Living!

Lurking in the shade of a tree, wondering how he can possibly sneak in, Matthew catches an unusual noise. A sort of hum, getting closer. Matthew flattens himself onto the pine needles that litter the ground ... A glimpse in the curve of what was once a road, a ... truck! The word itself is now almost obsolete; the tech-nology unused for so many years! A covered truck! The vehicle approaches and passes a few meters from Matthew, who sees pas-sengers. There are women sitting in the back; Matthew sees them clearly.

VIII.   Scientific Environmentalism

Human activities are estimated to have caused global warming of approximately 1.0°C above pre-industrial levels, with a likely value of between 0.8°C and 1.2°C. Global warming is likely to reach 1.5°C between 2030 and 2052 if it continues to increase at the current rate (high confidence).

IPCC, SR15, SPM, A1.

By the end of the twentieth century, environmentalism as a rational theory was nothing more than an anti-humanist ethic bristling with outdated scientific arguments. In short, a superstition.

The theory of anthropogenic global warming emerged.

This theory has been progressively asserted, thanks to an original institutional and normative phenomenon.

Until the 1970s and 1980s, it was not uncommon for the press to announce a new era, not of warming, but of glaciation. These are the same magazines that depict the Earth as a ball of melting ice, which showed us paralyzed on the edge of a Dantean ice floe.[41]

---

41 *"The Cooling of America"* December 1979, *Time*; *Newsweek* showed in April 1975, graphs in support of the inevitability of global cooling (*"The Cooling World"*).

The reason for this reversal can be spelt out in four letters: IPCC, the acronym for the UN Intergovernmental Panel on Climate Change. It is not necessary to enter into the genealogical and structural intricacies of this institution[42]; let us bear in mind only that the establishment of this diplomatic group was in response to the desire of the British government to acquire scientific approval of its predilection for nuclear energy (at the end of the 1980s.)[43] The focus of the IPCC is Man's influence on the climate—not Nature and Man—only Man.

The IPCC immediately began to work and prepare reports in three parts: summary of the climate science, harmful effects for Man, and measures to be implemented to remedy them.

It is often said that the problem with the IPCC is that the summary for decision makers erases the uncertainties of the report itself.

This criticism is well founded, but superficial.

The problem with the IPCC is that it claims to be scientific; "The IPCC is a scientific body" (see IPCC.ch); this is a false claim because, in every way—composition, authority, functioning—it is political and even diplomatic.[44]

However, the IPCC claims to *derive* the "recommended measures"—the third part of its reports—from a scientific summary of the first part, which is, at best, a naive and rationally primitive process. It is rationally impossible to derive a standard from a fact.

---

42.   See Laframboise, The Delinquent Teenager Who Was Mistaken for the World's Top Climate Expert, 2011.

43 "Thatcher & Global Warming: From Alarmist to Skeptic," https://www.masterresource.org/climate-exaggeration/thatcher-alarmist-to-skeptic/

44 See our *The IPCC: A scientific body?*, 2015.

For this reason, the rational value of the IPCC reports is zero. Not debatable, nor amendable: just zero.

This notwithstanding, the IPCC reports have been celebrated for 30 years by most western governments—with the notable exception of the White House, since 2016—as the voice of science. It is not the IPCC that observes and advocates: the very concept of science speaks through the mouth of the IPCC.

Since its second, and, especially, its third report, the IPCC has favored the theory of anthropogenic global warming, according to which Man, through his production of CO_2 (more generally, of so-called greenhouse gases[45]), causes environmental warming that will have deleterious effects.

Admittedly, according to the IPCC, humans emit only 4% of global CO_2 emissions: 96% are natural.[46] But by a so-called "radiative forcing" effect,[47] this slight surplus of human CO_2 upsets the natural balance and causes global warming.

---

45 From here on the term "CO_2" will be extended to include all greenhouse gases.

46 IPCC, AR5, figure 6.01.

47 "Radiative forcing measures the impact of certain climate-related factors on the energy balance of the coupled Earth/atmosphere system. The term 'radiative' is used because these factors alter the balance between incoming solar radiation and emission of infrared radiation from the atmosphere. This radiative balance controls the temperature on the planet's surface. The term 'forcing' is used to indicate that the Earth's radiative balance is being destabilized. Radiative forcing is generally quantified as 'the rate of energy transfer per surface unit of the globe, measured in the upper layers of the atmosphere', and is expressed in watts per square metre (…). A radiative forcing caused by one or more factors is said to be positive when it results in an increase in the energy of the Earth/atmosphere system and thus the warming of the system. In the opposite case, a radiative forcing is negative when the energy goes down, which results in the cooling of the system. Climatologists face the difficult problem of identifying all the factors that affect the climate, as well as the forcing mechanisms, quantifying radiative forcing for each factor and estimating the sum of radiative forcing for a group of factors": IPCC, Working Group 1, Frequently Asked Questions, FAQ 2.1, Box 1.

The atmosphere of early environmentalism remained fundamentally moral, despite efforts made for scientific approval; the new environmentalism wants to be scientific.

IX. The Two Advantages of New Environmentalism

If we do not reduce greenhouse gas emissions both rapidly and dramatically, we will not succeed. The scientists' message has been sent.

La Tribune, 8 October 2018

The theory of anthropogenic global warming has two inestimable advantages: first, it is readily comprehensible. Human CO_2 is the cause of global warming: a child can grasp this proposal. For the past 25 years, the AGW theory has been relayed in a thousand and one ways by the media, using a template that consists of linking human activity, even the most innocuous—eating meat, visiting a foreign capital, staying warm, having a child—with CO_2 emissions. With all human activity emitting CO_2, the media portrayal of the AGW theory is virtually unlimited.

Second, AGW establishes Man both as the cause of the problem and as its remedy. Because if human CO_2—4% of total CO_2—causes warming, then we *can* act, because human behavior is very much governed by law and morality.

Nature cannot be constrained but Man can be constrained in a thousand and one ways; history bears witness to this.

Initially a moral philosophy, environmentalism was transformed by the grace of AGW into a scientific theory with totalizing pretentions: both global in ambition and intent on pervading each and every gesture, activity, and action of the individual.

X. The Totalizing Analytic
of Environmentalism[48]

If you control carbon, you control life.

Richard Lindzen

Based on the theory of anthropogenic global warming, environmentalism is now emerging as a scientific theory, for which the empire extends scientifically to all things.

There is, in fact, not a single one of Man's actions or activities that does not generate CO_2. Transport, heating, buildings, industry, economy, and even the simple act of breathing; CO_2 emissions are consubstantial with the fact of existence, with the very concept of the human.[49]

"If you control carbon, you control life," noted the American physicist Richard Lindzen: upon this truth—a scientific truth— is the empire, totalizing in its principle, of contemporary environmentalism.

Authoritarian regimes have marred western history, but totalitarianism is a recent invention.

---

48 In the Kantian tradition, an analytic judgment is the one in which the predicate is inscribed in the definition of the subject.

49 Take a moment to read the summary of the latest IPCC Special Report (SR15) and ask yourself what human activity do the authors not desire to control, https://www.ipcc. ch/sr15/ {Hint: none}

The citizen of Sparta was accountable to the city for the most binding duties, from childhood to death. Sparta was a military camp, which entailed the hierarchy, control, and submission of the individual to the imperatives and views of the community. Sparta, however, lived under the rule of law and the separation of powers (Aristotle), thus providing the citizens with a share of freedom (the majority of the people were either slaves or of an intermediate category called the Hilotes). The Spartan regime was undoubtedly authoritarian and military, but it lacked the totalizing pretension of the abolition of individuality.

Many "absolute" monarchs desired to rule the individual, but they did not have the means, neither financially nor technologically (and rarely legally) speaking. Above all, the totalizing pretension was simply lacking. The effective empire of Louis XIV over the territory of his kingdom was paltry compared to that of our democracies.[50]

Totalitarianism is a contemporary invention, which emerged in the literature of the nineteenth century, before being implemented in the next century.

Fascism was essentially a nationalist form of socialism. Mussolini abolished the elections but left scattered elements of pluralism, including the monarchy. In the twisted workings of Hitlerian pathology, the German was but a cog. The National Socialist theory endeavored to conceptually destroy the "bourgeois individualism" of the Anglo-Saxon.

---

50 Totalitarianism should not be confused with despotism, defined as the submission of the individual to the whim of power. Despotism speaks of the absence of a law under which to hide from the whims of power; it does not in itself imply any totalizing pretension.

Through re-organizing the economic society, communism finally organized everything. Born in blood, communism governed arbitrarily. Mao's China, the Khmer Rouge's Cambodia, Lenin's and Stalin's USSR, all these regimes are numbering among the most "anthropophage" of history.

However, communist totalitarianism never planned or even *conceived* of subjecting human activity in its *entirety* to the sanction and control of the State.[51] In the USSR, people travelled as freely as the available means allowed, but travel or transport were never considered problematic *in themselves*. Holidays were taken sparingly, because the means of a planned economy were limited, but if the Party had had the opportunity, it would have increased such. Material comfort and consumption were not disqualified in principle, only by the limitation of the capacities of the "red" economy.

Homo Sovieticus was tightly policed, oppressed, and materially limited, when he was not being deported in the Gulag and killed. However, he was never considered by the Party and the State as a problem in himself: in his very humanity.

The divergence of environmentalism from previous examples of totalitarianism is not marginal: it marks an ontological turning point.

If human CO_2 is the problem, then Man is the problem.

---

51 Sigmund Krancberg, "Controlling Individual Development and Behavior," *Studies in Soviet Thought*, vol. 27, no.4, May 1984, pp.319-334.

The Mystery Thickens

"I am nothing, All is all"

Surpassing Humanity (collective work), 2031

This is what Matthew says to himself, after he manages to slip quietly into the women's truck, thanks to his small size. One of the women, who unfortunately does not speak his language, helps him to climb up to her side, after overcoming the surprise of seeing him scurrying behind the truck.

The women all resemble his mother, just before her Humusation: dilapidated with an air of resignation, as if already absent from their own bodies. Bleak incarnations of despair ... Not only do they not speak to him, but they do not speak to each other. Do they share the same language?

The truck enters the Nomenklatura of Resources without hindrance.

Seen from the inside, the Nomenklatura complex resembles the Ancient Cities described in books. Lights everywhere, paved roads, trucks and vehicles of all kinds, and unusual chimneys. Noise, noise everywhere. Matthew has never experienced such a cacophony stopping his mind thinking.

Spotting a kind of embankment alongside a building, the child jumps from the truck and hunkers down. The women watch him passively and continue on their way.

XI. Environmentalism and freedom?

*The battle for the climate is contrary
to individual freedoms.*

François-Marie Bréon, climatologist[52]

Coercion? Perhaps, but coercion in a good cause.

The Population Bomb, Paul Ehrlich[53]

Thinkers such as Hans Jonas risk advocating a benevolent environmentalist autocracy,[54] in the interest of the planet. Environmentalists venture to argue for the abolition of the political freedom that is democracy. No environmental party already advocates the abolition of freedom as such.

Freedom was both invented by the west and is the catalyst and crucible of its development. Conceived by the Greeks, with the concept of *isonomia* (Solon) or equality before the law, taken up

---

52 https://www.liberation.fr/planete/2018/07/29/francois-marie-breon-la-lutte-pour-le-climat-est-contraire-aux-libertes-individuelles_1669641

53 *op. cit.*

54 Jean-Marc Gancille , *Ne plus se mentir - Petit exercice de lucidité par temps d'effon-drement écologique,* {*Do Not Lie Anymore - A Little Exercise of Lucidity During a Time of Ecological Collapse* } RUE ECHIQUIER, 2019.

and shaped by generations of Roman jurists and publicists; then in Common Law, by the tradition of the German *Rechtsstaat*, the Anglophone Rule of Law, the Francophone état de droit, there is freedom only under the auspices of true law, with definite, fixed, and thus avoidable sanctions. Freedom is diametrically opposed to arbitrariness. Economic freedom is intrinsically linked with the market economy and ensures the perpetuation of its various manifestations, including technological progress.

In spite of a century of socialism, our culture remains imbued with the demand for freedom: that value, which is the very condition of morality (Kant).

Demanding the abolition of freedom hardly seems likely to bear fruit and most environmentalists do not. Moreover, environmentalists know that the same objective can be achieved by apparently less radical means. Didn't a thousand small restraints keep Gulliver from moving, as if he were paralyzed from the neck down?

How can we escape environmentalist theoretical mechanics? If human CO_2 is the problem, then human being's many activities are the problem. Will the individual be allowed to go about his or her business as long as CO_2 emissions are inherent to each of them?

Freedom = CO_2

Thus, freedom is being at liberty to emit CO_2, which no coherent environmentalist can tolerate.

The theoretical system by which environmentalists would seize our societies does not allow them to escape this conclusion: in its principle or its applications, individual freedom must be abolished.

Let us consider two identical populations. In the first, individuals are free to move, start a family, trade, travel, eat meat, and own pets. In the second, individuals are not free and only allowed activities prescribed by the central authority, for example by issuing CO_2 emission licenses.

How can we deny that the second group will indeed emit significantly less CO_2 than the first? How can we fail to see that environmentalist theory forces us to qualify the second group as virtuous, whereas the first is harmful, selfish, and "abuse the planet"?[55]

To eliminate ("by 95%") human CO_2 emissions, it is necessary to abolish individual freedom.

In this way, the totalizing analytic of environmentalism induces a totalitarian algorithm:

If human CO_2 is the problem, then humans must be restrained, controlled, and conditioned in each of their activities.

In an interview with *Der Spiegel* in 1992, Hans Jonas reached the same conclusion: in view of the "ecological catastrophe" and the "technological attacks on Nature," "the renunciation of individual freedom is *inevitable*."[56]

---

55 Aurélien Barrau : "Pourquoi a-t-on encore la liberté d'agresser la planète ?," {"Why do we still have the freedom to abuse the planet?"}, https://www.nouvelobs.com/planete/20180928.OBS3121/aurelien-barrau-pourquoi-a-t-on-encore-la-liberte-d-agresser-la-planete.html

56 Italics added. *"Dem bösen Ende näher,"* {"Closer to the evil end"}, *Der Spiegel*, 11 May 1992.

XII. An Ambitious Totalitarianism

Civilization is killing the planet.
Civilization must be destroyed.

Derek Jensen, *Endgame, Vol. 2, Resistance*, 2006[57]

At first glance, environmentalism is a coherent theory; due to his productivism, Man emits ever more CO_2. This CO_2 causes global warming that will ultimately make the planet uninhabitable. So, we have to act before nature collapses, because then it will be too late.

One reencounters the theme of the tipping point, constant since Malthus, and the idea of a phenomenon that will take place in such a way that we must intervene in advance because, afterwards will be untimely.

It should be emphasized that contemporary environmentalism does not derive its totalitarian impulse from morality, but from science. When that science, as reported by the IPCC, focusses on the literally destructive and maleficent role of human CO_2, it is natural for those who are concerned about mankind to look at every human activity that emits CO_2, that is, the entirety of Man's actions, from his first to his last exhalation of CO_2.

57 Seven Stories Press.

In short, environmentalism is a totalitarian Frankenstein's monster that has escaped its creators; if human CO_2 is the problem, then Man is the problem. Relativizing this proposition forces us to renounce the theory of anthropogenic global warming, thus returning to the moral environmentalism that is so weakly built on scientific pretext.

As we see from its stated motives, environmentalism is more demanding, more radical, and ambitious in its desire to subdue Man than any previous doctrine.

Perhaps the closest parallel exists in the *panopticism* of Michel Foucault, on the model of the *panopticon* prison by Jeremy Bentham. Bentham's *panopticon* is a prison structure that accommodates the guard in a central tower around which the prisoners' quarters are arrayed so that they are constantly observable, without them knowing when they are actually being observed. Then the control, in action and power, is *total* (permanent). In *Discipline and Punish: The Birth of the Prison* (1975), Foucault generalized panopticism, defined as a desire to impose, through social control, the required conduct on a target group.

One must look to the dystopias of science fiction to see similar representations of total control. The environmentalist pretension, however, is not fictitious.

The totalitarian radicalism of environmentalism can be seen in its identification of "the enemy." Totalitarianism thrives thanks to the enemy. Let us remember the kulaks and other "revisionists" in Stalin's worldview; or the National Socialist regime's perspective on the Jewish community.

Environmentalists do not single out any particular community. Of course, they do not approve of the bourgeoisie, the "rich," or the haves[58] but there are no kulaks in environmentalist theory, any more than there are "bourgeoisie" in the sense of Karl Marx. There are only greenhouse gases.[59]

Neither kulaks nor bourgeois; this is because the enemy of the environmentalists is elsewhere. He is in all of us. The enemy is *us*, playing our part in CO_2-producing humanity, that is to say the totality of who we are.

From that departure point, a gradation of responsibility (and the degree of hostility): the westerner produces more CO_2 than the Sub-Saharan African, the White more than the Black, the "rich" more than the poor. He who lives in a detached house will emit more than he who is satisfied with a more modest dwelling.

The enemy is in each one of us and no one is deemed innocent; the enemy is in Man, in our species, in the very fabric of our relationship with the world.

The enemy is Man.

---

58 Sociologists such as Bertrand Hervieu ("Recours à la ruralité et crise," *Économie rurale*, n°140, 1980, pp. 16-20, with Danièle Léger) and Hubert Billemont ("L'écologie politique : une idéologie de classes moyennes.," *Political ecology: a middle-class ideology*, University of Evry-Val d'Essonne, 2006) maintain that environmentalism is first and foremost the result of less-well-performing middle-class universitarians, those who have achieved at best mediocre academic results. Billemont refers to them as "a semi-intellectual fraction of the working middle class."

59 The term "greenhouse gases" will be used in the rest of this work, without it being seen as a concession to this or that theory or as a challenge. Let us note, to attest to the debate, that Prof. Georges Geuskens, Phd, DSc, of the University of Brussels (ULB) argued in an article published on 14 February 2019: "The theory of anthropogenic global warming based on the existence of a greenhouse effect has no theoretical or experimental justification." http://www.science-climat-energie.be/2019/02/14/le-rechauffement-climatique-dorigine-anthropique/

XIII. Marxism and National Socialism's "Excessive Language"

*Popular revenge on hated individuals
must be encouraged and directed.*

Karl Marx[60]

Every theory, doctrine, or religion has extreme followers, and it is a mistake to attribute the errors of the few to the doctrine when they are foreign to the essence of the doctrine in question.

A careful study of national socialist literature shows that the abominations finally perpetrated were predictable and even announced as early as the 1920s. In a speech *Warum sind wir Antisemiten* (*Why we are anti-Semites*) delivered in 1920, five years before *Mein Kampf*, Hitler theorized the foundations of his vision of the world, and his abhorrence of the Jews, irreconcilable with a national socialist regime.

In this widely disseminated speech, Hitler explains that he is, first of all, a socialist and defines socialism as an egalitarian ethic. He goes on to explain that true socialism can only be established within the confines of one nation, the German nation, and one race, the Aryan race. Finally, Hitler concludes by explaining that, as a socialist, he must reject the opposing worldview, that is, materialism and Jewish mammonism.

---

60 "Ansprache der Zentralbehörde an den Bund vom März 1850," *Anhang IX der Enthüllungen über den Kommunistenprozess zu Köln*, Zurich, Hottingen, 1885, p.79.

All are common themes in the literature of National Socialism, borrowing greatly from Marxism, and of which most of the authors came via theoretical socialism. In the 1920s and 1930s, these rationalizations of anti-Semitism were often regarded as imprudent rhetorical excess, which was attributed to nationalist fervor, existing rancor, the outbursts of Hitler, and other exogenous factors.

Yet, these "excesses" were neither peripheral nor transgressive in relation to the essence of National Socialism; on the contrary, they revealed the truth. National Socialism put to use established anti-Semitic hatred that was present in German culture at the time. What is more, it reinvigorated it with theoretical justification. As it theorized the legitimacy of the expulsion of the Jews by a German socialist society, Hitler's socialism offered a theoretical alibi for the homicidal urge of anti-Semitism.

The same is true of Marxist literature. Generations of scholars have endeavored to argue that Marxism was, in practice, as deadly as National Socialism, but, nonetheless, in some way, morally superior because the murderous hatred of Nazi theory is absent in that of Marx.

A careful study of Marx's writings suggests that this is not the case. The surprisingly unrecognized Marxian concept of *Volksrache*[61] conveys the idea that after the revolution—with the revolutionaries victorious—the party must not oppose the destruction of the symbols of the defeated regime, that is, the monuments, the goods, and the members of the hated bourgeoisie. Marx explains that this popular rage (*Volksrache*) should not be fought, but channeled and even encouraged.

---

61 *La passion de l'égalité,* p.91.

A sanction for legal lynching and slaughter; this was the fate of many members of the "bourgeoisie"—those who were judged to be such—who were massacred during and after the Bolsheviks took power in Russia, as they were in many communist countries.

The condoning of legal lynching by Marx could be discounted as rhetorical excess, like other elements of the Marxian theoretical corpus, but only while Marxism was mere rhetoric. As soon as it was put into practice, the evidence arose that this sanctioning of violence, never denied by Marx, was of the essence of Marxism.

XIV. Environmentalism's "Excessive Language"

Gradually extinguishing the human species by voluntarily ceasing to reproduce will allow the biosphere to recover its health.

Movement for the voluntary extinction of humanity[62]

At a conference given in September 2018,[63] French astrophysicist Aurélien Barrau, a member of the steering committee of the Centre for Theoretical Physics of Grenoble-Alpes University and the ENIGMASS laboratory of excellence and the French National Committee for Scientific Research, explained that Man is problematic for nature and that our destructive behavior (for "macrofauna") is unfortunately inherent, not only in what we do, but in what we *are*: voilà the totalizing analytic and physisistic ethics as previously identified.

The problem is ontological, according to Mr Barrau. Man, explains our physicist, is a weak creature, unable to reason on the "collective scale": in short, a sick being. Therefore, we need practical, coercive, unpopular political measures that counter individual freedom. We no longer have the choice to do otherwise. This is a shocking message, but consistent with the essence of new environmentalism.

---

62 http://vhemt.org/index.htm

63 https://www.youtube.com/watch?v=R7sMZiSKmqg

In an interview with *Libération* dated July 29, 2018, French climatologist François-Marie Bréon of the Laboratory of Climate and Environmental Sciences (French: Laboratoire des Sciences du Climat et de l'Environnement, LSCE) and IPCC author, explained that it is imperative we give up heating and tourism, shut down entire parts of our economies and finally renounce individual freedoms and democracy; all realities that are incompatible with the fight against CO_2 emissions. Even these measures will still be insufficient, stated the distinguished climatologist. This is because the only way to preserve the environment will be to reduce humanity by a factor of ten. Unlike the abovementioned Mr Ehrlich, Monsieur Bréon is yet to specify how we rid ourselves of nine-tenths of humanity.[64]

Incidentally, this is what we have dubbed the humanicidal temptation of environmentalism,[65] an urge wholly consistent with its theoretical foundations.[66]

The ideal Earth for environmentalists is the Moon.

---

64 The desire to reduce humanity to a tiny fraction of current levels has taken an obsessive turn in environmentalist literature, which produces *"ideal"* figures all the more fanciful since they neither rest *nor can rest, even in theory* on any rational basis. When the American ecofeminist Lierre Keith argued that the ideal number for humanity would be no more than 8 million individuals, up pops a pundit, the *Biosphère* blogger, to estimate that it is still too much and that one must go down to *"one to two million."* http://biosphere.blog.lemonde.fr/2017/11/16/la-terre-ne-peut-porter-que-1-a-2-millions-dhumains/

65 *Contrepoints*, 11 December 2018.

66 By the way, when *Libération* journalist Sylvestre Huet called for "the suppression of the rich" in the name of the climate, he showed both the powerful egalitarian vein of environmentalism and its grossly murderous penchant. https://twitter.com/HuetSylvestre/status/1107923954969133057

XV. The Noble Lie of Environmentalism (Hans Jonas)

*We must "overcome the liberal
naivety of public veracity."*

Hans Jonas, *The Principle of Responsibility*[67]

How can we make humanity accept its eradication?

In *The Republic*, Plato develops the theory of the "noble lie," which differs from the "true" lie in that it is uttered in the interest of its recipient.

To be justifiable, this lie can only emanate from the one who governs and must be in the interest of the city:

"It is, therefore, up to those who govern the city, if indeed, such is conferred on certain individuals, to lie, whether to enemies or to the citizens, in the interest of the city. For everyone else, it is out of the question to use it."[68]

Plato gives examples of noble lies. For example, the myth of autochthony, which would have it that the citizens were all born of Mother Earth (*sic*) and that they are, therefore, brothers (and sisters). However, so that each citizen remains in his place, the "noble

67 op. cit., p.203.

68 II, 389b.

lie" will allege that various metals intervene in the composition of beings—gold, silver, and bronze—and that those who are made of gold are destined to govern, silver will be guardians, and bronze, merchants.

In short, everything is good as long as the ruler believes that the lie is in the interest of the city.

This interesting theory is echoed by a twentieth century environmentalist thinker, Hans Jonas:

"Perhaps the dangerous game of the mystification of the masses (Plato's 'noble lie'), is it the only route that politics will ultimately offer:[69] to allow the 'Fear' principle[70] and to hold sway under cover of the 'Hope' principle. But that presupposes the existence of an elite and clandestine intentions, and its accession in a doctrinal totalitarian society is more implausible than under the conditions of an independent formation of opinion in a free society (or among individualists)."[71]

This is a remarkably revealing passage, which considers that disinformation will flourish and take root better in the context of "free" information than in the model of centralized—and therefore suspect—information familiar to authoritarian regimes.[72]

Jonas continues: "Certainly in the case of utopia we also say that, under certain conditions, the most useful opinion is false opinion, which means: if the truth is difficult to bear, the pious lie must intervene."[73]

---

69 Jonas is aware of the difficulty of imposing insecurity through democratic means.

70 Prefiguration of the precautionary principle.

71 *The Principle of Responsibility.*

72 See our *La réalité augmentée,* 2011.

73 Jonas, *The Principle of Responsibility.*

The thesis of this spiritual father of contemporary environmentalism is as "Platonic" as it is clear; if it is necessary to lie to citizens to make them accept the renunciations, the ontological degradation, the panoptic control, and the insecurity inherent in the environmentalist plan, not only is this lie possible, it is noble.

Smoked

"Why persist?"

Thanatos in Love, 2032

Matthew tucked himself between the outer wall of a large building and a pile of bags full of organic waste. From this refuge, he sees, emerging from the other end of the complex, high chimneys spewing greasy fumes.

Matthew's knowledge of science is almost non-existent. The teaching of that subject had been strongly discouraged for years, because it was technological innovation that had led humanity into the impasse of Hypercarbonization (the Fossil Era).

However, Matthew knows there is no smoke without a fire, such as those that his father lights during the frequent blackouts. (In 2049, the only heat is renewable electricity, the intermittence of which regularly compels the citizenry to scavenge for wood.)

Between his position and these chimneys, Matthew distinguishes a long line of barracks, which seem to be made of timber. The young boy soon finds out that the truck he had climbed into was not the only one in the Nomenklatura and that various vehicles were circulating around the barracks and coming in and out of the gate.

Matthew is hungry; he is afraid and wonders what he is doing there. Finding evidence of Isabelle and her family seems unimaginable. What can a 12-year-old child do in this huge complex of which he understands nothing, neither how it works, nor even why it exists? Why does this complex resemble the cities of the past? What are these chimneys, the likes of which were abolished years ago?

What can he do?

XVI. Attempt to Understand the All Living

Gaia is alive.

Clive Hamilton (2013)[74]

We must concede a certain transcendence to Nature.

Hans Jonas (1991)[75]

Let us accept the environmentalist premise of the All Living.[76]

Does this All Living have the capacity of reason? Can it express feelings?

No, of course it cannot, and the very question will be taken as "anthropomorphic," i.e., interpreting life from the point of view of Man.

Let us, therefore, concede that this All Living is devoid of reason and sentiment.

---

74 *Requiem for a Species: Why We Resist the Truth About Climate Change*, Routledge, 2010.

75 Interview with *Esprit*, 1991, p.15.

76 This is the Gaia Hypothesis formulated in 1970 by James Lovelock in *Gaia: A New Look at Life on Earth*.

Is the All Living corporeal, forming an identifiable and distinct whole?

No. Because the All Living is not a mammal, reptile, or bird.

Perhaps the All Living is characterized by lesser motility and sensitivity, a particular chemical composition, or a nutrition based on simple elements (i.e. a plant)?

No, not that either.

Is it an amoeba?

The amoeba is an organism.

The All Living can be alive only in a sense that is literal and without any scientific reference. If the All Living is alive, it is, by definition and necessity, in a sense that does not fall within any scientific category.[77]

If the All Living is alive, it can only be so by a unique modality that transcends science and the living world.

If the All Living is alive, it is God.

---

77 See Richard Dawkins, *The Extended Phenotype: The Long Reach of the Gene*, Oxford University Press, 2016: Gaia does not "replicate," so does not exists as a "living entity."

PART TWO—APPLIED ENVIRONMENTALISM

In this second part, we will see how environmentalism rolls out the totalitarianism of its algorithm in every aspect of real life.

XVII. Environmentalism and Democracy: A Broken Marriage

> Democracy (…) is not the appropriate form
> of government in the long term.
>
> Hans Jonas (1992)[78]

Although it is not easy to gain power through promises—there is tough competition—it is virtually impossible to get the majority vote if offering only harassment, constraint, and privation.

We have noted a difference between socialism and environmentalism; while the former promises abundance, the latter guarantees insecurity. Elective, noble, moral, and even scientific, but insecurity, nonetheless.

It is, therefore, hardly surprising that the environmentalist parties remain minority parties and that they have, to our knowledge, never received an absolute majority in any election in any western country.

---

78 *"Den Verdacht habe ich, daß die Demokratie, wie sie jetzt funktioniert - mit ihrer kurzfristigen Orientierung - auf die Dauer nicht die geeignete Regierungsform ist."* {*"I suspect that democracy, as it now works - with its short-term orientation - is not the appropriate form of government in the long term."*}, interview with *Der Spiegel*, 1992, https://www.spiegel.de/spiegel/print/d-13680535.html

Environmentalists occupy 9% of the seats in the European Parliament, a modest and relatively constant percentage of which significant growth cannot be predicted.

Yet, the influence of environmentalists, in law and in fact, far exceeds their parliamentary representation. How is such a phenomenon possible?

It is because, without winning any national election, environmentalists have mastered ideological lobbying and the colonization of places of power at an international level.

The United Nations, the IPCC, the Council of Europe, the European Court of Human Rights (ECHR), the Court of Justice of the European Union (CJEU): so many small and undemocratic cadres with such real power. International law is not black or white; it is nuanced. Little of international law is binding in the strictest sense. Its influence is somewhat marginal, for instance, in being invoked by judges in justifying a decision. However, by cumulative effect and by self-reference, this quasi-law or proto-law ends up achieving strict legal force.

When a standard is derived from one of these cadres, two scenarios arise. Either the standard is mandatory or applies in each of the national constitutional systems, overriding national law. It is widely recognized that the international standard outweighs the national standard. Put another way, when the international standard is adopted, it is, thus, positioned beyond even the reach of national parliaments.

When the standard is not mandatory as such, it has been noted that it can *become* so, for example by being utilized by lawyers and judges, if only to interpret the actual law. An example is the endless proliferation of UN resolutions and recommendations. This is an apt example because international law is *comprehensively* taking precedence over national law. Provided that a modest legal effect is recognized to a quasi-rule of international law, it will wholly prevail over national democratic law; the judges will ensure this.

There are entire sections of the law that are being progressively put out of the reach of national democracies and their parliaments.

The case of the IPCC is both composite and of great interest. The third section of the IPCC report is certainly not legally binding; it does not apply with the force of law in our national legal systems, nor does it override, as such, any national regulation. However, this catalogue of "proposed" norms is so detailed and extends so well to all spheres of human activity—transport, town planning, construction, economy, tourism, national and international redistribution of wealth—that it is a ready-to-use, off-the-peg product. To be convinced, one only needs to read the third section of the third and fourth IPCC reports; note that many of these "recommended standards" have entered into law.[79]

The case of the European Union is no less singular; here is an international organization that adopts directives and regulations, strict legal norms that prevail over national parliaments. Due to its intense regulatory activity—European law is comprised of 160,000 pages—the EU is depriving national parliaments of significant portions of their powers. National democracies are being stripped of their powers that are brought to the institution, the EU, which is fundamentally intergovernmental and undemocratic. This normative alienation is one of the proven causes of the British vote in favor of Brexit.

It is probably at the EU level that the green lobby has become most fully institutionalized:

---

79 See our *The IPCC: A scientific body?*, 2015.

"The European institutions are working with many partners and interest groups to help them shape public policy, thus establishing a new model of governance. Among these partners are the 'Green 10', which works closely with the European Commission for the purpose of advice, expertise, and assistance in the development of European environmental policies. (...) The 'Green 10' is the assembly of the 10 largest environmental NGOs active at a European and international level.[80] They assist European policy makers in the development of their policies and are crucial partners in terms of environmental expertise. These organizations receive direct support from the European Commission's Environment DG, which partly funds[81] their actions and supports their projects."[82]

Environmentalists cannot triumph by democratic means any more than they would be able to maintain their position by democratic means; hence, they favor the intergovernmental approach of international law.

In the long term, its totalitarian algorithm condemns environmentalism to consider a form of dictatorship and tyranny, a plan in which a significant number of environmentalist intellectuals are already actively involved.[83]

---

80 Among them Greenpeace and Friends of the Earth, radical environmentalist organizations subscribed to so-called "deep ecology."

81 So much for the "non-governmental" nature of NGOs financed by governments.

82 Sciences-Po Strasbourg, https://mastereurope.eu/contentgreen-10-les-ong-vertes-a-bruxelles/

83 Charlotte Belaich, *"Accept that freedom stops where the planet begins,"* *Libération*, April 2, 2019 and the many references cited in the discussion, including Gilles Boyer, Michel Terestchenko, Dominique Bourg and Kerry Whiteside, Thomas Schauder, Michel Tarrier, Luc Semal.

XVIII. Indecent Pluralism

Climate: "Enough Talk, Act"

Open letter from environmentalist associations to the French government[84]

Pluralism poses no problem as long as debate continues between socialists and liberals, nationalists and supporters of the European Union, or atheists and supporters of Christian humanism. It is even a kind of stimulus, in that pluralism obliges the refinement of argument and vigilance in the face of the adversary's contradiction. These ideologies have integrated the moral, philosophical, and constitutional imperative of pluralism, and have applied it for many decades in both Western Europe and the United States.

The debate freezes as soon as an opponent enters the political/media arena sporting the bedazzling armor of science. Not of "humanity," but the "hardest" science, the science of exact and pure objectivity: physics!

Then, the debate is no longer between different moral considerations that are, and will remain, fundamentally relative and subjective. The debate rages now between morality and science! Well, not exactly "rages" for how could the relativity of ethics face the objectivity of science? How can we contradict, discuss, debate, and hope, in some way to refute physics with morality?

84 https://www.ritimo.org/Climat-Assez-de-discours-des-actes

This fact has not eluded the environmentalist parties, which behave like so many walking IPCC reports. Here is science, and from science we derive the following imperatives: (see the manifesto of whichever environmentalist party concerned). Science imposes environmentalism. We are science; what about you?

A formidable combination and a formidable transcendence of the "scientific" argument in the political debate! We are returning to the dream of scientists à la Renan, in the nineteenth century:[85] a government of and by science!

As soon as we accept the scientific pretensions of environmentalism, pluralism becomes unthinkable and even repugnant. How can one tolerate a moralist "debating" climate physics?! Will there be discussion of the survival of humanity?

However, this is all based on a misunderstanding.

Renanian scientism—government by science—has never been put into practice. Not because of Man's wickedness or his appetite for superstition, but because it is a logical impossibility. A simple fallacy.

We have already touched on the subject; science holds the kingdom of fact. Its mission is to bring to light the laws that govern the physical world, even the strange case of the laws of quantum mechanics! Science is Western Civilization's prodigious progeny and its principal catalyst—thanks to technological progress. Its kingdom is unassailable, but should she exit this kingdom, science is nothing; she has nothing more to say. A Physicist-Monarch, resolving to govern by science regardless of subjective considerations, would simply be unable to make *any* decision, talk, or act!

---

85 Ernest Renan, *L'Avenir de la science*, {*The Future of Science*},1890 (written in 1848): "Organizing humanity scientifically is therefore the right of modern science, such is its bold but legitimate claim."

Law, politics, and morality hold sway in the kingdom of moral values. From a thing—from a proposition of fact—one can never conclude (derive) an obligation. David Hume showed all this as early as the eighteenth century, in works reprised and extensively developed by Hans Kelsen.[86]

Let's take an example. Smoking harms health. It is a fact; the research leaves no doubt on the subject. Where does that lead us? Nowhere. Some will decide to smoke, because hedonism is more appealing to them than living a long and healthy life. Others will abstain from smoking and dedicate themselves to sport, which brings other pleasures and probably a longer life. Because there is a rule, there is a qualitative leap, which lies in the values that one decides to implement.

Rule = Fact + Value

Science informs regulation; it informs the decision-making process. Yet, it is powerless to replace it.

As this intellectual fallacy is somehow embedded in the very structure of the IPCC and its reports, it defines the relationship of scientific environmentalism with the world. The IPCC claims to *derive* recommended standards (Part 3) from the Climate Science Summary (Part 1). In the strictest rational sense, not a single normative proposal, even if formulated as a suggestion, can be derived from science: not a word, not a comma.

If environmentalism is a science, it has no say in the political field; if it goes there, it ceases to be a science.

---

86 See Hans Kelsen, *General Theory of Law and State* and our "Clôture ou pique à bestiaux ? À propos du concept de norme générale chez Hans Kelsen," Arguments, *European Journal of Science*, vol. 1, #1, Fall 2016, https://www.academia.edu/32194542/ Cl%C3%B4ture_ou_pique_%C3%A0_bestiaux_%C3%80_propos_du_concept_de_ norme_g%C3%A9n%C3%A9rale_chez_Hans_Kelsen

XIX. The "Noble Lie" in Journalism

*The environment is a debate that goes
beyond any political consideration.*

Anne-Sophie Bruyndonckx, RTBF journalist[87]

As soon as the survival of the Earth is at stake, many journalists believe it is legitimate to abandon objectivity: to exercise their activism.

Fear and catastrophism have become the norm in the handling of the "climate" topic by most elements of the media, with two driving factors. First, because of the disproportionate success of the environmentalist ideology within the ranks of journalists,[88] far greater than amongst the public at large. Second, because catastrophism sells and is an inexhaustible vein of editorial inspiration.

The use of fear in the climate debate is validated in the academic world. In a contribution, "Fear Appeals in Climate Change Communication," published online under "Climate Science," Oxford Research Encyclopedias, in September 2017, Joseph P. Reser and Graham L. Bradley wrote: "Extensive research literatures addressing preparedness, prevention, and behavior change in the areas of public health, marketing, and risk communication

---

87 https://www.rtbf.be/info/inside/detail_ce-dimanche-certains-journalistes-avaient-climat-eux-aussi-les-journalistes-des-manifestants-comme-les-autres?id=10087732

88 In Francophone Belgium 46% of journalists voted in 2013 for the environmentalist party: https://www.levif.be/actualite/belgique/la-presse-francophone-est-elle-trop-a-gauche-place-a-plus-de-pluralisme/article-opinion-1054347.html

generally (...) provide consistent empirical support for the qualified effectiveness of fear appeals in persuasive social influence communications and campaigns." In summary: fear works.

Yet, catastrophism is not the only exploitable vein on the theme of climate.

In an interesting synthetic contribution, "Post-normal Journalism: Climate Journalism and Its Changing Contribution to an Unsustainable Debate"[89] published in 2017, Michael Brüggemann utilized an example of militant post-journalism, which has become the norm of the profession regarding the climate:

"An example of such an approach is the Guardian's 'Keep it in the ground' campaign, calling for divesting funds from fossil fuels. The campaign combines transparent advocacy and innovative storytelling. It was kicked off by an editorial and complemented by traditional reporting and a podcast that also provided a glimpse into the newsroom. The Guardian clearly acknowledged its partnership with the NGO 350.org. While this is another instance of the blurring boundaries between journalism and activism, it is also an act of creative journalism that deliberately focuses on new angles from which to cover climate change. With its more recent focus on solar energy, the Guardian also provided an example of what has been called 'constructive' or 'solutions journalism' (...). It seems that this is another shift away from 'normal' journalism with its focus on negativity that provides conflict and damage as strong news factors. (...) While such a mission runs contrary to the model of the detached

---

89 Peter Berglez, Ulrika Olausson, Mart Ots (Eds.): *What is Sustainable Journalism? Integrating the Environmental, Social, and Economic Challenges of Journalism*, New York, Peter Lang, pp.57–73.

observer, the severity of the climate problem may justify the exception, in the view of at least some of the world's leading climate journalists (…)."

"Is the climate 'universal'?" asked RTBF, the Belgian public-service broadcasting organization:

For journalist Anne-Sophie Bruyndonckx, among others, the answer is yes. She defines herself as first and foremost a citizen and believes it normal and healthy that a journalist should engage in society. "I think it is important to remember that we are part of this society on which we report, she said. There are subjects that seem universal to me: I want to say that I am opposed to violence against women and to racism, there is no debate to be had on this." For her, the climate is just as important: "We have arrived at a time when the planet is not well, we all have to be careful, and that is a fact that we talk about in our newspapers, there is nothing to discuss. The environment, in this sense, is a debate that goes beyond any political consideration, any boundary, any status – boss, employee or freelancer, whether you are black, white or yellow.[90]

Post-journalism, creative journalism, "solutions" journalism, constructive journalism, or citizen journalism; there is no shortage of expressions to describe what, strictly speaking, is no longer journalism, but militant activism in the service of the environmentalist ideology.

Let us look at the relationship between environmentalism and economic theory.

---

90 "I can't, I have a climate": journalists, joining the protesters? , RTBF, https://www.rtbf.be/info/inside/detail_ce-dimanche-certains-journalistes-avaient-climat-eux-aussi-les-journalistes-des-manifestants-comme-les-autres?id=10087732

An Intriguing Smell

"sssssshffffffffrrrrkkkkhhhouuuu (an ant singing)"

Arne Trunbull, *Human Stain*, date unknown

Matthew notices children—children! —walking amongst the alleys of the Nomenklatura, seeming to enjoy a relative freedom of movement. He decides to step out from his cover, doing his best to appear calm.

Matthew sets out towards the chimneys; they loom overhead dominating the complex. He soon passes two young girls who must be two or three years older than him. He returns their smile and slips on by. Getting closer, Matthew catches the stench of the chimney fumes.

Why does the Nomenklatura, of all things, resort to such an ancient, outdated, and polluting process?

That's when Matthew is intercepted.

XX. The Non-existent Economy

I've never considered myself an economic expert.

Hans Jonas (1992)[91]

From Karl Marx to Lord Keynes, socialism has spawned powerful theoretical systems, with real conceptual innovations. For example, the *General Theory of Employment, Interest, and Money*, published by Keynes in 1936,[92] masterfully collated the many economic elements into a new conceptual apparatus.

Despite extensive research, it has not been possible for us to identify a single environmentalist author who specifically proposes a novel economic system, not even a reworking of existing concepts and formats. Environmentalist philosophies, environmentalist morals, political programs, even an environmentalist macro science,[93] most definitely, but as for a proposed economic system? No.

This is hardly surprising, as economic nonexistence is consistent with the theoretical foundations of environmentalism.

---

91 Interview with *Der Spiegel*, https://www.spiegel.de/spiegel/print/d-13680535.html

92 A coherent socialist, as evidenced by the moral and practical primacy which he recognized in the egalitarian imperative, Keynes was the spiritual father of democratic socialism after 1945.

93 Etopia, https://etopia.be/introduction-a-la-philosophie-economique-et-politique-de-lecologie/ and our *The IPCC: A scientific body?*

Socialism is an "economism," in that everything is subordinate to the imperative of material equality.

Environmentalism is not an economism, because it is defined by its rejection of the economy. From the Meadows Report (1972)[94] to contemporary environmentalism, passing by the so-called alter-mondialism, it has been as if, tired of their failings in terms of theory, the opponents of the market economy now confine themselves to demanding that it be stopped.

The only economic concept that can reasonably be assigned to the environmentalists is negative economic growth.[95]

Negative economic growth is the idea that we should not increase our economic output, but reduce it; not encourage trade, but reduce it; not improve productivity, but set it aside.

All ideas that don't make a system. To make a system—that is to say to offer a theory, a rational plan—a *General Theory of Negative Economic Growth*, should answer the question of how. Negative growth, certainly, but how? How can economic production be reduced? Which sectors of the economy should be eliminated? Should technological progress, as such, be prohibited, or only its economic applications?

Economic growth means the growth of domestic economic output. As a nation declines, it bears less fruit, a phenomenon observed during major economic crises. The question is: which citizens,

---

94 "No one can predict what sort of institutions mankind might develop under these new conditions." (p.174)

95 The "circularity," which consists in favouring closed loops through recycling, would only make a system if it could be generalized to *all* economic activity, which no environmentalist supports. In the present state, circularity consists of adding loops to a system whose Nature and content are not changed; loops which can, moreover, be seen as benevolent from the point of view of economic rationality.

individuals and families will see their standard of living reduced? Maybe the elderly, through pensions? Or the "rich," the middle class, or everyone? Is it necessary to introduce a "license to pro-create" to achieve rapid and drastic population reduction?

It is not a matter of arguing that decline is not the goal of environ-mentalists: it is. However, it is a matter of arguing that that does not constitute an economic system.

XXI. Greening the Law

*Any government decision that could reasonably
have an impact on the climate or climate policy
must undergo, in advance, an impact assessment.*

Draft of Belgian "Special Climate Law"[96]

Since the climate topic is a question of survival, environmentalists demand that law, value, and enterprise are subordinate to it.

This leads them to plead for the adoption of laws and constitutional arrangements expressly aimed at placing climate at the heart of the decision-making process, so that no legislative, executive nor judicial decision, is taken that has not been measured in terms of its effects on "the climate" (read: CO_2 emissions).[97]

By constitutionalizing "the climate," environmentalists force judges and constitutional courts to balance civil liberties with the climate imperative. This means, in practice, that the exercise of a freedom is granted, recognized, and protected by the law *only*

---

96 http://www2.usaintlouis.be/public/comcom/presse/proposition_de_loi_speciale-fr.pdf

97 In Belgium, Article 3 § 2 of the *"climate law"* proposal—now abandoned—provides that *"Any government decision, which could reasonably have an impact on climate or climate policy must be subject to a prior assessment of this impact."* It is true to say that *every* decision *without exception* is concerned, for there is no conceivable decision, which has no impact in terms of CO_2 emissions. Full text: http://www2.usaintlouis.be/public/comcom/presse/proposition_de_loi_speciale-en.pdf

if the CO_2 emissions are deemed "reasonable and proportionate," according to the criteria familiar to the lawyers specializing in public law.

The emergence of the climate into the constitutional arena is an evident paradigmatic shift; it is the logical and predictable juridical continuation of what we have called the totalitarian environmentalist algorithm.

In addition, European environmentalists demand that "climate committees"[98] are set up to advise each level of power in their consideration of climate factors, through regular recommendations and reports. The quasi-normative mechanism that has been so successful at the IPCC is readily recognizable.

It is palpable that this "balancing" of civil liberties and climate demands is just one more step toward a new "civilization."

Knowing that there are no activities or actions of Man that do not emit CO_2—from the smallest movement to warming our homes—it is foolish to brandish individual freedoms in the face of the collective survival of humanity. Raising the "right" to move, on a whim for frivolous purposes, when the future of mankind is in peril?

The tension between freedom and climate is a mere preamble to the ultimate goal of this environmentalist juridical and judicial revolution: the subordination of freedom to climatic demands.

Be it in their moral philosophy or legal technique, we repeatedly encounter the inexorable character of the totalitarian algorithm of ecology: if human CO_2 is the problem, then Man in the infinite variety of his actions must be constrained, restricted, and tamed.

---

98 Article 9 of the Belgian climate law (not adopted), *op. cit.*

XXII. The Children's "Climate" Crusade

"Climate: A Global Strike Orchestrated by Children"

Franceinfo, March 14, 2019[99]

Although convinced of the superiority of their cause, the pre-AGW environmentalists generally speaking respected certain limits; they were never seen using young children in any of their actions.

The new environmentalists do not recognize the legitimacy of these limits.

Now that the survival of humanity is at stake, all means are acceptable and even just; the imperative is both moral and scientific.

Now we see that environmentalists no longer hesitate at having teenagers and even children take to the street "for the climate." In Flanders, in January 2019, there was a demonstration "for the climate" of children from nursery school—from 3 to 5 years old—taking up, in chorus, the political slogans of their elders.[100]

99 https://www.francetvinfo.fr/meteo/climat/climat-une-greve-mondiale-orchestree-par-des-enfants_3233081.html The article does not problematisize in any way the title and thus validates the idea that this "world strike" was indeed organized by the children themselves ; including authorization to demonstrate, financing, transport, demands.

100 *"Fanatisation of childhood, a modality of abuse?"*, *Le Vif*, 31 January 2019, https://www.levif.be/actualite/international/la-fanatisation-de-l-enfance-une-modalite-de-l-abus/article-opinion-1086345.html

Comparisons naturally come to mind. For example, the *Komsomol*— those Soviet communist youth organizations— although the Soviets wouldn't allow kindergarten children to enroll; or the Children's Crusade, the lunacy of children fanaticized by adults who ended up being slaughtered by the opposing forces; or consider the enlisting of German youth by the National Socialist regime, the *Hitlerjugend.* In these three cases, we find the identical stratagem of the ideological subjugation of childhood.

In Flanders, kindergarten and primary school children were *obliged* to participate in these events (as part of their compulsory schooling), even if this was contrary to the opinion of their own parents. This politicization of childhood, contrary to the family's wishes if need be, is not common in our democracies.

Can we imagine schoolteachers forcing four-year-old schoolchildren to demonstrate for capitalism, socialism, or Christianity? Why does what is absolutely unthinkable become legitimate when it comes to environmentalist ideology? The legitimacy of contemporary environmentalism rests on moral considerations, like any ideology and doctrine, but that this ideology mesmerizes with the alleged endorsement of science radically distinguishes it from its rivals.

This comparative advantage allows it to nurture global ambitions and demand that the obstacles—freedom, economy, pluralism, and childhood—which stand in its way, be dismantled without delay.

Does the survival of humanity not deserve certain sacrifices?

Let us now turn to the phobias of environmentalist ideology.

Face to Face with the Co-President of the Nomenklatura

1. Ecocide (Crime by Humanity)

Nomenklatura of Criminal Justice, date unknown

It is his shoes that betray him: Matthew's, like those of all the people of the valley, are much the worse for wear, while those here in the Nomenklatura are new. When approached and ordered to state his Nomen—the number assigned by the Nomenklatura— Matthew was unable to do so and was immediately taken to an interrogation room.

Under questioning, Matthew blames his escapade on curiosity: after all, they're not telepathic they can't know his real intentions. He says nothing of Isabelle and her family.

Soon, Matthew is put in solitary confinement in a small cell in the heart of the large building against which he had sheltered.

***

Two days later, a gender-neutral comes to his cell, to announce that he will be received by the Co-President of the Nomenklatura. Matthew is unaware of this title and what it might entail; he has no choice but to follow the wo/man.

After an interminable journey through the building, Matthew is brought before the Co-President and left alone with her. She is a woman of modest appearance, dressed in a neutral manner, without ostentation, affable. It is she who starts the exchange:

— *I am told that your curiosity has brought you to us?*

— *Yes.*

— *It's dangerous to do that. You could have hurt yourself. Next time, why don't you present yourself at a gate?*

Matthew is chastened, rendered speechless.

— *I'm not hiding the fact that I have to make a difficult decision about what we're going to do with you. Either I let you go back to your father—your mother was humusated I am told—or I keep you with us.*

— *I prefer to leave.*

— *Ah but, my young friend, things are not that simple. We found you in the north of the compound, didn't we?*

— *...*

— *Near the chimneys.*

— *Yes, by the chimneys.*

— *What other places have you visited?*

— *None. I was afraid of getting caught. Why not let me go?*

The Nomenklatura Co-President paused as if about to make a declaration of principle before answering the question.

— *Let you go?! But, my friend, what world do you live in? Do you not know that Humanity has entered the era of Great Reparation to allow the planet to regenerate by the drastic reduction of the CO_2 of the pestilent creature? Are you ignoring ...?*

— *I know all this.*

— *So, you know that, in their last report, the IPCC scientists estimated that it would take several centuries to return to sustainable CO_2 concentrations. You know that we have entered the era of the Restorative Fallow, which offers many opportunities, but certainly not the freedom to come and go at will!*

Matthew does not know what to say. Then, in changing the subject, he reveals himself:

— *Where are the women who came into the camp with me?*

— *We are not a camp! We are the Nomenklatura, the modest stewards of resources for the duration of the Great Reparation.*

— *Where are the women who came into the Nomenklatura with me?*

— *My young friend, I doubt you are able to understand these matters. It is enough for you to understand that some people refuse to adapt to the imperatives of the Reparation and that they persist in anti-Gaian behavior.*

— *Such as?*

— *Having children, starting families ... For example.*

— *I've seen children here!*

— *We must ensure the perpetuation of the Guardians of the Fallow. Without Guardians there would be no reparation. We are bound by our own rules.*

Matthew says nothing. After a few moments, the Nomenklaturist repeats:

— *Give me two days to reflect, and I will decide your fate.*

XXIII. Environmentalist Phobias

For the climate, please avoid the car, meat, and children.

Lorrie Goldstein[101]

Ideally, we should abandon the plane. Give up your personal car, do nothing but walk, cycle, take public transport. And therefore, live in urban centers.

Mélanie Gelkens, *"The World in 2050"*[102]

Let us see where the totalitarian algorithm of their doctrine leads environmentalists in addressing the detail of the entirety of human activity.

---

101 *Toronto Sun*, 15 July 2017.

102 *Le Vif*, no.16, 18 April 2019.

The Plane

Let us Google "Global Warming Plane Trip." Notice the results: "Can we still travel by plane if we have an environmental conscience?" ; "Flying shame: Greta Thunberg gave up flights to fight climate" ; "For the climate, we must stop taking the plane"; "No longer taking the plane is being visionary"; " How your flight emits as much CO_2 as many people do in a year" ; "To save the climate, do we have to give up the plane?"; "Air Travel Emissions: Worse Than Anyone Expected" — is it possible? — "For the climate, would you be willing to sacrifice your air travel?" ; "Climate change: Should you fly, drive or take the train?"

The plane takes us at will to the four corners of the world, and it is said that "Travel broadens the mind." Thanks to its democratization, air travel is no longer the privilege of the "rich." It was not long ago when intercontinental travel was a display of wealth!

This democratization—the low-cost travel, so hated by some among the "elite"—was one of the greatest successes of the European Union,[103] back when it was content to be a common market facilitating trade and freedom.

Alas, aircraft consume kerosene and emit CO_2. In the great environmentalist mono-factorial metric, it is, thus, necessary to reduce its use and access, that is to say to return to the *status quo ante*, that of its use being reserved for the wealthy.

The case is all the more interesting because it is characterized by the clash of two contradictory logics. On the one hand, the logic of encouraging trade—that is, the Convention on International Civil Aviation, which was signed in Chicago in 1944 to facilitate trade,

---

103 Samuel Furfari, *Ecology in Wonderland*, p.205 of the French Edition.

prohibits States from levying taxes on aircraft fuel[104] (planes are taxed in many other ways). On the other hand, the environmentalist logic of penalizing air travel and discouraging it as much as possible, by forcing travelers to pay "much more"—according to one Belgian minister—for their air travel.

The plane is consubstantial with the globalization of trade, in all areas, not only the economy. Until the assertion of "scientific" environmentalism, the availability of international travel was seen not only as an economic benefit but also of intellectual, cultural, and of true moral benefit.

Sweden, always ahead of the curve on these issues, has brought in the "flygskam" initiative, which aims to morally stigmatize those who travel by plane—whatever their motives may be—in their first step to prohibition.

There is nothing here that is not consistent with the totalizing analytics of scientific environmentalism—the fight against human CO_2—even though, in this regard, as in all others, scientific justification gives substance to previous demands.

104 "Fuel, lubricating oils, spare parts, regular equipment and aircraft stores on board an aircraft of a contracting State, on arrival in the territory of another contracting State and retained on board on leaving the territory of that State shall be exempt from customs duty, inspection fees or similar national or local duties and charges." (Article 24)

Centralization by the Government of all Means of Transport

Environmentalists view the automobile as one of the most repugnant manifestations of freedom ever created.

The term "automobile" refers not only to private cars, but also lorries and all kinds of private vehicles.

The first reason for this phobia, claimed and demonstrated, is pollution. Cars pollute: that's true. However, technological progress has allowed these pollutants—we are talking not about CO_2 but pollutants: SO2, lead, CO, NO2, PM10 particles, and benzene—to be reduced to almost nothing.

"So what?" retorts the environmentalist community, saying that there are more and more cars; even if each of them pollutes less, as a whole, they pollute just as much, and we still have pollution.

This is not exactly true. First, because the number of vehicles in most Western countries is stabilizing; second, because the *overall volume* of pollution measured is insignificant compared to what it was 30 or 40 years ago.[105]

Certainly, private transportation emits CO_2, but how can we conceive that substituting public—government-run—transportation will lead to a reduction in global CO_2? Does history and economic theory not teach us that interventionist methods are less efficient, consume more resources, and are more polluting than the alternative system, that of the freedom of economic actors? How can we

---

105 Christian Gérondeau, *L'air est pur à Paris... mais personne ne le sait !* (*The Air is Clean in Paris... but no one knows it!*), Paris, L'Artilleur, 2018.

imagine an efficient allocation of "transport" resources in a government-run system which, by definition, is deprived of the price mechanism?[106]

All other things being equal, it is certain that, for an identical volume of transport, a public system will be less efficient (much less) and emit more CO_2 (much more) than a system with complete freedom to move and transport.

This transition from unlimited private transport to public transport only makes sense if travel is drastically reduced and here lies the *raison d'être* of this call for the collectivization of transport, not for the better allocation of resources, but to gain greater control by that act over the citizenry and the economy.

Environmentalists are not joking when they advocate for a complete change of economic and political system; careful planning and control are on the menu.

This, again, highlights the astonishing methodological parallels between environmentalism and Marxism. The title of this chapter is not borrowed from an environmentalist thinker. It is an exact quotation from the *Communist Manifesto* of Friedrich Engels and Karl Marx.

Let us now examine three specific proposals, which indicate that the elimination of human CO_2 is not the ultimate goal of environmentalists and that anthropology plays its part in the background, dictating priorities, at the expense of tackling greenhouse gas emissions.

106 Ludwig von Mises, *Socialism*, 1922.

Meat

> *It shouldn't be the consumer's responsibility to figure out what's cruel and what's kind, what's environmentally destructive, and what's sustainable. Cruel and destructive food products should be illegal.*

> Jonathan Safran Foer, *Eating Animals*

From the Flemish party GROEN to the French state think-tank NOVETHIC, passing by the "Green New Deal" proposed legislation sponsored by Rep. Alexandria Ocasio-Cortez (D-NY) and Sen. Ed Markey (D-MA), environmentalists demand that meat consumption be rationed,[107] in line with the "recommendations" of the IPCC.[108] A study by the Oxford Martin School in 2016 indicated that the propagation of vegetarianism would reduce greenhouse gas emissions from meat consumption by 63.1%.[109]

---

107 "What the Green New Deal will mean for your hamburger," *The Guardian*, 7 March 2019.

108 SR15, SPRM, p.18.

109 And even 70.3% with a vegan diet: http://www.oxfordmartin.ox.ac.uk/downloads/academic/160317_Springmann_co_benefits_data_overview.xlsx : "climate change analysis" tab.

The claim is surprising. Of course, meat production, and the cattle themselves emit CO_2, but it has been shown that if we had to produce alternatives to feed humanity—e.g., lab-grown or synthetic meat—it would generate comparable or even significantly higher CO_2 volumes.[110]

If the fight against human CO_2 emissions truly is the *ultima ratio* of environmentalism, why attempt to penalize meat?

The explanation is simple: since long before the theory of anthropogenic global warming came about, environmentalists have refused to recognize the primacy of Man common to most doctrines, ideologies, moralities, philosophies, and religions. Those who distinguish between the nature of Man and that of the animal are accused of speciesism. In France, the word "Specists" has been found daubed on the facades of bemused butchers blissfully unaware that such is the mark of Cain.

What is important to note here is that there is an imperative in environmentalism, a more fundamental motivation than the fight against CO_2: an ethic, an underlying anthropology.

---

110 In reality, lab-grown meat is still only at the research stage; its incubators, which consume large amounts of energy, can only produce a few grams of *"meat"* at present. See E. Dolgin, *"Sizzling Interest in Lab-grown Meat Belies Lack of Basic Research," Nature*, 6 February 2019: *"Clean Meat' firms have drawn tens of millions of dollars in investment in recent years, but technical hurdles remain."*

Modern Agriculture

When we see land as a community to which we belong,
we may begin to use it with love and respect.

Aldo Leopold, *A Sand County Almanac and Sketches Here and There*

The same ambivalence is evident with regard to agriculture. Environmentalists not only demand that agriculture emits less CO_2, they want to ban "deep ploughing," the use of pesticides and fertilizers, and modern irrigation techniques. In other words, they want to ban modern agriculture.[111]

Of course, modern agriculture emits CO_2. However, per ton of produce, modern agriculture emits significantly less CO_2 than traditional agriculture.

Two explanations are possible: first, environmentalists want to drastically reduce the volumes produced by agriculture; a return to rudimentary methods while emitting less CO_2 is then thinkable. But then the question immediately arises as to who will go hungry? How will we segregate the categories? How will we identify them, sort them, select them, and who will be condemned to hunger?

111 *Soil Atlas—Facts and Figures About earth, Land, and Fields*, Heinrich Böll Foundation, Berlin, Germany, and Institute for Advanced Sustainability Studies, Potsdam, Germany, 2016.

Let us remember that, putting the rhetoric and slogans aside, there are human lives at stake. If India or China, for example, gave up modern agricultural technologies to return to traditional methods, it would immediately plunge hundreds of millions of people into famine. This was the reality in these countries before the "green revolution," that is to say, the development and sharing of modern agricultural methods and technologies.[112]

The second possible explanation, which is not incompatible with the first, is that the fight against CO_2 is only a pretext to serve other ends.

112 Guy Sorman, *Le progrès et ses ennemis*, Paris, Fayard, 2001.

Nuclear Energy

Nuclear energy is both expensive and dangerous.

Greenpeace USA[113]

While the reduction of CO_2 emissions seems to constitute the alpha and omega of all things environmentalist, its claims, and *raison d'être*, let us highlight two countries that suggest that, behind the fight against human CO_2, lurks another reality.

France emits one of the least CO_2 per capita in the OECD.[114] The reason for this is the country's historic preference for nuclear power, which produces 75% of its electricity. Nevertheless, environmentalists across all their parties demanded and obtained that France embark on a costly "energy transition" following the German model, also called "environmental transition" (environmentalists never write "environmentalist", always "environmental"; it is science that speaks, not ideology).

This transition to so-called renewable energy, in practice intermittent energy, will in no way improve France's carbon footprint. It is, in fact, materially impossible to produce less than zero, and nuclear power does not emit CO_2.[115]

---

113 https://www.greenpeace.org/usa/global-warming/issues/nuclear/

114 Organisation for Economic Co-operation and Development, an intergovernmental economic organisation with 36 member countries.

115 Taking into account the energy production as such but also the life cycle of a nuclear power plant—from the extraction of the raw materials to the storage of waste—the CO_2 emissions from nuclear power are comparable to those of renewable energy.

The hatred of nuclear power that environmentalists nurture must surely be motivated by something other than the will to reduce CO_2 emissions.

The case of Belgium is even more telling. Here is a small country that produces 50% of its electricity through nuclear power. Under pressure from environmentalists, this country decides to abandon it completely—without consultation —by 2025, taking out of service, all at once, its seven nuclear reactors. Four of these fully-paid-off reactors could continue to produce low-cost, zero-carbon electricity for years to come.

To replace this zero-carbon energy source, the environmentalists called for the construction of power plants with... gas. That is to say, fossil-fuel power plants that emit infinitely more CO_2 than nuclear power.

The realization dawns that, not only is there something other than the will to reduce CO_2 emissions at play, but that this ulterior motive, fundamental to the environmentalist approach, is decisive and overrides the will to reduce "anthropogenic" CO_2.

XXIV. Altruistic Euthanasia

*Not caring for the elderly is no longer a
question of cost, but of quality of life.*

Corinne Ellemeet, Dutch environmentalist politician[116]

When Corinne Elisabeth de Jonge van Ellemeet, Member of the
Dutch Environmentalist Party "Groenlinks," makes the reduction
of treatment for those over 70 years old a *sine qua non* of govern-
mental negotiations,[117] it may look like a personal, marginal, and
deviant agenda. After all, "reducing care for the elderly," in plain
language, means death. Rationing care—and that is what it is—is
nothing less than letting people die.

Looking at it closely, we will see that her proposal is in no way an
isolated case in the environmentalist *Weltanschauung* (vision of
the world); it is taken up and shared by many associations, think
tanks, and environmentalist parties.[118]

116 "Het gaat mij niet om de kosten, maar om de kwaliteit van leven.," *De Telegraaf*, 13 February 2019,
https://www.telegraaf.nl/nieuws/3151780/minister-aan-de-slag-met-omstreden-plan-groen-links

117 "Wrede GroenLinks-troela Corinne Ellemeet wil ouderen zorg afpakken: Stoppen
met 'overbehandelen'!" ("Cruel GroenLinks Simpleton Corinne Ellemeet Wants to Take
Care' of the Elderly: Stop 'Overtreatment'!"), *De Dagelijkse Standaard*, 12 February
2019, https://www.dagelijksestandaard.nl/2019/02/wrede-groenlinks-troela-corinne-el-
lemeet-wil-ouderen-zorg-afpakken-stoppen-met-overbehandelen/

118 "Health: Is it Acceptable to Discontinue Treatment for the Elderly?," *Le
Soir*, March 19, 2019, https://plus.lesoir.be/213081/article/2019-03-19/
sante-est-il-acceptable-decesser-les-traitements-pour-les-plus-ages

Moreover, this suggestion to let nature do her work is consistent with a "pattern," which is to see the older person—or indeed the individual—as first, and foremost, a consumer of resources and emitter of CO_2.

An unthinkable practice 30 years ago, in direct contradiction of the Hippocratic oath, euthanasia recently arrived with a fanfare into the law of several European countries. Safeguards have been erected, but the principle is clear: when a person decides that his life is meaningless, he may put an end to it.

Euthanasia—or suicide—has always existed and is part and parcel of being human: since time immemorial, some have preferred to end their own lives. What was inconceivable, until recently, was to legalize the practice—to *normalize* it—because people go through "rough patches" and experience lapses of strength that leave them vulnerable.

Such concerns have been swept away, and in countries like the Netherlands and Belgium, legal euthanasia—legal killing—of those who request it is now considered normal.

The main argument of the supporters of euthanasia—which is far from anathema to classical liberals—is that those who are euthanized do so of their own free will. Yet this argument does not stand up to analysis.

Indeed, the debate has moved on to the extension of euthanasia to persons who are no longer able to express their own free will.[119] That is, persons who, by definition, do not now express and may have never expressed the desire to be euthanized.

---

119 Frank Judo, "Euthanasia Legislation in the Netherlands and Belgium: More to it than meets the eye," Laennec, 2013/2, volume 61, pp.69-79.

What is more, Belgium has recently legalized the euthanasia of children—regardless of their age—even before the ability to express consent, or in fact to express anything, has been gained.

Euthanasia is now legal without the consent of the human subject.

The demands of the Dutch environmentalist politician follow in this vein, since they demand the limiting of care to all the elderly, regardless of consent, a small step towards containing the "rampant apocalypse" that is humanity.[120]

The careful consideration of environmental pseudo-anthropology—which is little more than a metaphysic of Nature, as Hans Jonas would have it—gives astonishing insight.

120 Hans Jonas, interview with *Esprit*, 1991, p.11.

Matthew meditates

In the confinement of his cell, Matthew meditates. There's not much else to do, except the physical exercise, which he forces himself to perform. Matthew just turned 13, but no one thought to wish him a happy birthday.

Matthew wonders how previous generations saw the world. How a child—a young teenager—of his age might have seen the world, the past, his future. Matthew can only see the aftermath of the upheaval.

It all began in a minor way, and under the benevolent eye of science. It started by drastically reducing car traffic before banning it by collectivizing transport. The crime against humanity of denying Man's depredations of Nature was made law. Article Zero, the Climate Article, was given precedence in the European Convention on Human Rights, the imperative of the survival of humanity overshadowing civil liberty. The new article was rapidly adopted in most national constitutions. Environmentalist economic planning offices were soon set up to ensure that no economic initiative or activity took place that contributed in any way to global warming. In France and Belgium, Article 544 of the Civil Code, which enshrines private property, was not repealed as such but was somewhat supplemented. "Property is the right to enjoy and dispose of things in the most absolute manner, provided that they are not used in a way prohibited by the laws or statutes" became "Property is the right to enjoy and dispose of things within the limits of the law and climate imperative." High-speed internet—what was then called 5G—was outlawed, in the name of public health and the preservation of resources.

The combined effect of these measures was called Environmental Deceleration, and, soon, the Age of Modesty. Unfortunately, this modesty did not last, because soon after, the economy collapsed and the unrest grew.

Increasingly violent disorder justified the establishment of a state of emergency. Pensions went unpaid, social security benefits were scrapped, the courts ceased to function, and travel and heating became difficult since everything had been electrified and the national energy grid had collapsed under the weight of its own costs. The elections were postponed, then suspended, and never reinstated.

Faced with the threat of chaos and anarchy, the ineffective national administrations were gathered together in a European Sustainable Economy Plan, with national "chapters."

Matthew does not know the details; when his father speaks of that time, he does so with passion and even fervor. All Matthew knows is that due to the European Sustainable Economy Plan and the establishment of the Nomenklatura of Resources, the population of his village shrunk by 80%, and he is now the only child.

How did we get here? How can we justify that the Nomenklaturists live in luxury—luxury that Matthew had thought only possible in the bygone era—while he and his fellow men are poor. Yes, poor! Miserable even! Everything rationed: water, electricity, heating, CO_2... Where am I now?

"Why?" thinks Matthew. "Should I solve it? Am I nothing? Just another resource? Is there nothing in me that justifies a form of ...? The child cannot find his words.

He awaits the verdict.

XXV. A child = 58.6 Tons of CO_2 Equivalent (tCO_2e) Per Year

The population explosion should be
stopped; it must be stopped!

Hans Jonas (1991)[121]

The mother of the year should be a sterilized
woman with two adopted children.

Paul Ehlirch, *Life*, April 17, 1970

In an article widely circulated in the press, "The Climate Mitigation Gap: education and government recommendations miss the most effective individual actions," published by *Environmental Research Letters* in 2017,[122] the authors advocate three ways to reduce greenhouse gas emissions: universal veganism, rationing of air travel, and giving up the car. Although worthwhile, the authors stress that these three methods have little impact relative to the ideal: "having one less child." This is justified by an estimated sum of the tonnage of CO_2 emissions that is the trademark of such literature.

---

121 Interview with *Esprit*, 1991, p.14.

122 Seth Wynes and Kimberly A. Nicholas, *Environ. Res. Lett.*, (2017), p.12.

Birth phobia is probably the subject which best demonstrates the soul of environmentalism—'deep ecology'—and its real nature.

It is no secret that, for several decades, the fertility rate of western women has been below the replacement rate. Westerners are no longer having enough children to maintain population levels. The phenomenon is only mitigated, and sometimes overcompensated, by the practice of immigration to an extent that is causing significant economic and cultural hardship: but that's another matter.

Historically, this drop in fertility was concomitant with the legalization of abortion, without there necessarily being a causality in this correlation, let alone it being unique.[123]

There are many difficulties with population decline. Let us mention only two; from an economic point of view, a declining market is generally synonymous at best with stagnation, and usually economic regression. There is also the problem of the payment of pensions, particularly in socialized countries with pay-as-you-go pensions, where pensions are paid not from a pot but directly by the working population. Should the labor force shrink while the retired population continues to grow? The situation quickly becomes unviable.

So many regressive phenomena end up affecting what may be called the morale of a nation. If a nation knows that it is ageing and shrinking it "feels" itself dying. With the current fertility rates in Western Europe, it will only take a few generations for the population to shrink by 70%.

---

123 The link between the two matters did not escape Paul Ehrlich: if we were to reduce the birth rate by half, it would be by instituting free abortion. Abortion is a radical means of demographic control, in *The Population Bomb*, op. cit.

It is against the background of this demographic collapse that many environmentalist think tanks are nonetheless proposing we have fewer children.

Why? Because a child—a human being—emits CO_2. Therefore, in the environmentalist *mathesis universalis*—which only addresses one criterion: CO_2 emissions—giving life becomes a problematic, regrettable and, to say the least, harmful act.

There is no environmentalist phobia about children, as such, but about the act of giving birth, that is giving birth to a source of CO_2.

One child = 58.6 tons of CO_2 equivalent (tCO$_2$e) per year.[124]

How could environmentalism escape its own postulates?

---

124 Seth Wynes and Kimberly A. Nicholas, *op. cit.*

General conclusion

It is the people who enslaved themselves,
who cut their throats.

Etienne de La Boétie, *Discourse on Voluntary Servitude* (1549)

If human CO_2 is the problem, then Man is the problem.

Whichever path we choose, theoretical or practical measures, contemporary environmentalism brings us back to this truism, this obvious truth. If human CO_2 is the problem, then Man in every activity, endeavor, action, and ambition is the problem.

It is worthless to object that the "polluting" industries are the issue at hand and not individual and daily activities.

Transport is one of the main causes of human CO_2 emissions. Such statistics are only the sum of a multitude of individual choices. Container carriers that sail from one continent to another are the materialization of individual free choices and the imposing incarnation of human activity at large. The same applies to heating, construction, and other human sources of CO_2.

If given free rein, human activity generates CO_2. It is intellectually impossible and practically inconceivable to isolate those human activities that emit CO_2, those that could be curbed and suppressed, and those deserving of carte blanche.

To compensate for past CO_2 emissions, Man must not only moderate current emissions, he must reduce them to nothing; the IPCC hath spoken. Certain political parties, in the afterglow of that IPCC bombshell, no longer hesitate at advocating the reduction of CO_2 emissions by 95% within 20 or 30 years.[125]

This objective can only be achieved by utterly dispensing with human freedom, for:

Freedom = CO_2

This is what we called the totalitarian environmentalist algorithm:

If human CO_2 is the problem, then Man must be controlled, restrained, and brought to heel in each of his gestures and activities.

This totalitarian algorithm shows itself in the environmentalist academic literature, as the demands of environmentalist organizations, and as the practical proposals of environmentalist parties. Totalitarian proposals, which suggest, recommend, and demand that Man be restrained in each and every activity: travel by car, travel by plane, meat consumption, energy, pet ownership,[126] euthanasia, (un)caring for the elderly, and even not giving birth and forced sterilization.

---

125 In accordance with the four maximalist scenarios of the latest IPCC report, SR15, cfr. *infra*.

126 "Dogs and Cats, Greatly Responsible for Global Warming," *Le Point*, August 3 2017. Such articles are typically based on academic literature, in this case G. S. Okin's "Environmental impacts of food consumption by dogs and cats," *Plos ONE*, 12(8), August 2017.

Despite notable similarities, and approaches that are at times "green on the outside, red (i.e., socialist) on the inside," environmentalism cannot, in any way, be considered a mere sub-branch of socialism. The socialist anthropology and the environmentalist "anthropology"[127] differ radically, as do their practical goals.

Of course, the similarities are important, both in motivation and method. Egalitarianism, which defines socialism, is no stranger to environmentalism. As a method, the totalitarian control of human activity is common to both Marxism—through a planned economy—and environmentalism.

Marxism, in its principle (its theoretical structure), is humanistic, because Man is the measure of all things, and nature is defined, problematized, and conceptualized only in its relation to Man. However, environmentalism recognizes the primacy of something greater, of Gaia-Sophia, the "All Living," nature in its entirety. Gaia! Man is envisioned by environmentalism only in light of his relationship with nature; the primacy returns to Nature. The Man of the humanist tradition is "the insular man" of environmentalism: an "impossible island," an error of perspective that must be overcome.[128]

Environmentalism and Marxism are also distinguished by the fact that Marxism is productivist, preaching equality in abundance, while environmentalism is anti-productivist. In Marxist theory, the means of production are seized to improve them and distribute their fruits equally. In environmentalism, the means of CO_2 production are seized to abolish them. Hans Jonas, environmentalism's great

---

127 There is no environmentalist anthropology in the strict sense, only a "metaphysic of Nature" (Hans Jonas), according to which Man is just another mammal, which is singled out only by his ability to harm the All Living (the first "Gaia" hypothesis of Lovelock).

128 Etopia, https://etopia.be/05-limpossibilite-dune-ile/

twentieth-century thinker, perfectly understood and highlighted this "ontological" difference between Marxist and environmentalist approaches.

Environmentalism is characterized by the antagonistic logic typical of totalitarian ideologies. However, the enemy it designates is not external; he does not reside in a category of the population defined in racial or socio-economic terms. The enemy, according to ecology, is in each one of us: it is *us*. This brings us back to the first conclusion of our work.

Their antagonistic logic is revealed in the "excessive language" of environmentalists, as it was revealed in the first speeches of German national-socialists and in the writings of Marx. Dictatorships have a history of announcing the dread atrocities they intend to perpetrate. Channeling the anti-Semitic prejudice, common among his countrymen at that time, Hitler and the national-socialist theorists built a theoretical foundation to this prejudice. It was valuable because it allowed the anti-Semite a rationale for his hatred; it structured a justification; it ennobled those smoldering embers and the first spark. Hitler's brand of socialism could only be established at a race level, the Aryan race; it presupposed the expulsion of radically heterogeneous elements: the Jews. The theoretical dynamics of Marxism are similar, although the racial element is not present, the "bourgeoisie" being in place of the "Jews."

When environmentalist theorists argue that democracy and individual freedoms are irreconcilable with the fight against anthropogenic global warming, they validate the first conclusion of this work. Their argument is consistent with the theoretical framework of environmentalism, which, if taken seriously, leaves no room for any alternative: to save Gaia, individuality must be abolished.

The perpetuation of a population level of 7.5 billion people is incompatible with the fight against global warming. To be 'green' and sustainable, and to move towards reducing human CO_2 emissions to zero, humanity should be divided—at least—by a factor of ten.

Dividing humanity by ten: this is the road map of contemporary environmentalism, rational and coherent with its postulates, its "physisistic" ethic and its pantheistic metaphysic. In response, it is not a plan; it is an observation, say some environmentalists. Ideally, we should reduce population levels, but, of course, it is impossible.

This objection does not stand up to analysis. The policy called for by environmentalists is to reduce *actually* human CO_2 emissions to nothing. They do not hesitate to voice this objective in international and national legal texts. Better than an abstract policy, it is then a strict legal *obligation*. The obligation can only be met, the plan carried out successfully, if humanity is, indeed, reduced to a fraction of what it is.

The environmentalist rejection of nuclear power and modern agriculture indicates that CO_2 and "anthropogenic warming" are actually pretexts. Environmentalists are fully prepared for CO_2 emissions to skyrocket as long as they serve their ultimate purpose, which is the subordination of Man to nature. It is interesting to note that the panoply of environmentalists' practical demands—banning meat, cars, and nuclear power; abolishing technology and the market economy; the reduction of humanity, if necessary by force—have not changed since *before* the theory of "anthropogenic global warming" was formulated.

Is the primary source of environmentalism not misanthropy?[129] Is the hatred of Man not the *Arche* (the first cause) of environmentalism, the only possible cause of all we've so far seen, in theory as in practical demand?[130]

From the roots of its "metaphysic of Nature" to the heady reaches of its practical demands, environmentalism is humanicide.

129 This is the conclusion in both *The New Ecological Order,* Luc Ferry, 1995, and Charles Rubin, *The Green Crusade: Rethinking the Roots of Environmentalism*, Rowman & Littlefield, 1998.

130 When Paul Ehrlich describes the genesis of his environmental awareness, on a certain summer night in Delhi, India, in an old-fashioned taxi, infested with fleas, surrounded everywhere by a mass of teeming men, men who defecated and urinated; men hanging on to buses; men herding their cattle; men, men, men, men, men... what does he describe if not his own physical repulsion tinged with racism?

The Forest Garden of Metamorphosis

"To die is to live"

GaiaMantra (fragment) unknown author, twenty-first century.

Now with clean clothes and his hair freshly trimmed, Matthew goes unnoticed: just another child. Again, he heads for the chimneys. Matthew wants to leave, to find his father, to be free now the Nomenklatura has shown itself to be merciful, but first, he wants to know.

During his confinement, Matthew summoned the scraps of history that he learnt from the school and his father. It is these scraps that allow him to make sense of the seemingly impenetrable enigma of his experience within the Nomenklatura.

He recalls how his teacher of the "History of the All Living" explained to him that technological civilization had reached a double apogee: American capitalism and German Nazism. Both of these regimes were characterized by the same obsession with technological progress, industry, and the same despoiling of our foster mother.

During the war—Matthew can't remember which one, a big war in the previous century—the Nazis conquered many countries. They had kidnapped their enemies and concentrated them in camps. Well, some of those camps didn't just detain the prisoners: they killed them. They gassed them. His last teacher of "History of the

All Living" had explained to them that this extermination was an example, among others, of the moral catastrophes of technophile civilization.

Matthew still recalls one image of a Nazi camp, in what was Poland ... long parallel barracks stretched as far as the eye could see ... the prisoners were locked up, waiting for their extermination.

These women who accompanied him to the camp ... these unusual chimneys ...

Matthew reaches the perimeter of the barracks, at the place where he was intercepted. No barbed wire or watchtowers: no need within the walls of the Nomenklatura itself. Women are engaged in small planting jobs. Once again, it is hot.

There are no guards, no dogs, none of the signs that Matthew associates with the camps he heard about at school. The occupants of the barracks seem to be free to roam.

Summoning all his courage, Matthew enters the second barracks on his right, between two identical and parallel constructions, surrounded by bare earth.

Inside, the air is heavy, loaded with various fumes. If there is running water, it has run a long way off. What strikes Matthew is the silence. Although hundreds of people—women only, no men and only a few children—seem to be huddling in this place, Matthew can hear very little being said. In addition to his own, Matthew hears languages he does not know.

The child finds, engraved on the faces before him, the same kind of resignation borne by the ladies who he had accompanied into the Nomenklatura. Sadness hangs in the air. No one seems to be interested in his presence, so he, too, chooses not to speak. He leaves.

Matthew does not know what to do; why aren't there any guards? Nothing fits. Could he have been mistaken? But then, why do these women live in these makeshift barracks, a few meters from the shiny buildings of the Nomenklatura?!

The child feels despair setting in. Lost in his thoughts, he trudges mechanically through the barracks, towards the chimneys. The atmosphere is oppressive. Is it the heat? Is it the fumes?

An old woman is sitting against the wall of a barracks. As he approaches, Matthew disturbs her reverie. She notices his presence, looks at him kindly, if a little vacantly. Matthew approaches her further; he greets her, she speaks his language.

— *What are you doing here, kid? I've never seen you before.*

— *I arrived recently.*

— *What do you want?*

— *I ... I want to know ...*

— *To know what?*

— *To understand what those chimneys are for.*

The exchange falters; the old woman seems so tired. But her warmth doesn't falter, her kindness, her protectivity almost loving.

— *You want to understand. Is there anything to understand? Do we always have to try to understand?*

— *Why are the chimneys for?*

The old woman looks at him smiling:

— *What's your name?*

— *Matthew.*

— *That's not a Nomen. You come from the outside.*

Matthew doesn't answer.

— *Don't worry. I come from the outside too.*

— *Why do they have chimneys? Why are there barracks? Who are these people? Who ... are you?*

— *What do you think the meaning of all this might be?*

Matthew repeats to her what his professors of the "History of the All Living" explained to him, although he struggles for the right terms, mixing up the fragments he learnt, the course of history swirling into a nonsensical farce.

At the end of his brief account, the old woman remains unresponsive. Her empty gaze fixed on him. Then Matthew sees a spark, which soon ignites into a twinkle, and the old woman begins to laugh. Her whole body, inert a moment ago, comes to life. She laughs as if her sides will split, gnashing at the air with her spoiled teeth. Calming herself down with great difficulty, the old woman barks out:

— *You think we're Nazis, don't you? You reckon these chimneys are for gas chambers? You think the Nomenklatura is some kind of extermination camp, like Auschwitz or Treblinka, don't you?*

Matthew doesn't know what to say; those names don't mean anything to him. The old woman repeats:

— *You little fool. Is that what you thought? You enter the sanctum sanctorum and defile it with banalities? How dare you compare the Nomenklatura to one of the most evil regimes of the Hubristic Era? Have you seen nothing? Understood nothing? Didn't your school teach you anything? Were your parents the ones who filled your head with these silly comparisons?*

Again, Matthew seems chastened. At the mention of his parents, he replies:

— *My mother died; she was humusated.*

The old woman starts to respond, then changes her mind; she gathers herself and takes another tack:

— *Why did she get humusated?*

— *Because she felt that her presence on our Earth was meaningless.*

— *Do you think she's the only one who comes to that conclusion? Don't you know that there are so many of them—so many of us—who share your mother's philosophy?*

She seems to have regained her temper and adopts an instructive tone:

— *During the fossil era, individuals lived as long as possible, beyond what was reasonable. It was not uncommon to live to a hundred. Called themselves centenarians! One hundred years of greenhouse gas emissions; one hundred years of resource consumption. Nowadays, we think that there comes a time, when the ... opportunities of existence are exhausted, when it is time to be welcomed back into our Mother's bosom ... To forget ourselves in the great All.*

This is the meaning of the complex you find yourself in, my boy.

— *But then, these people, these barracks ...*

— *All these people are here because they want to be. What you call chimneys, there, a few steps from us, is none other than the Access to the Forest Garden of Metamorphosis.*

— *What kind of metamorphosis?*

— *The mortal remains of humans represent biomass of far from negligible environmental worth. It would be a failure in the sustainable management of the environment not to have the proper reintegration of our remains into the biosphere. This Great Humusater that you have before you—for this is what it is all about—embodies our vision of life and death, in complete accord with the laws of Nature: we "come" from the Earth and, at the end of our earthly existence, we will return there as humus, living earth.*

— *I know all this.*

— *I know that, but let me round up. We're relics of a bygone era, our bodies are full of drugs, heavy metals, pesticides, fungicides, endocrine disruptors, nanoparticles, prosthetics, and so on. Only the purifying power of a properly managed super humusater can guarantee a return to Earth, with a clean slate, not even with one pathogenic germ, thus helping Future Generations. By choosing humusation, the only 100% environmentally friendly funeral practice, we stop poisoning the living with our mortal remains and reduce our overall ecological footprint rather than adding to it.*

— *But these women I saw in the barracks ... all these people... they are not sick. I saw some very healthy ones!*

— *Who are you to judge the meaning of their lives? Who are you to take away their right to stop polluting our Mother when they feel ready? What is important, their physical vigor or the maturity that they are exercising? Euthanasia used to be only for the desperate. The philosophy of our time is the opposite; choosing humusation is the apotheosis of the life of a humble and modest creature, respectful of the womb from which it sprang. Euthanasia was thought to be a kind of failure, a way-out; we see it as the ultimate act of love of a creature sacrificing itself for the well-being of the All. Millions of us made that choice here within our walls, and around the world.*

— *You ... you seem to know everything about this Great Humusater.*

— *I am its guardian. Do I seem like a 'kapo' to you?*

— *How does the humusation work?*

— *After removing the clothes and jewelry, the deceased is wrapped in a shroud made of a beautiful biodegradable fabric. A place is reserved for them in the Forest Garden of Metamorphosis for one year. The remains are placed on a cosy bed made of a skillful mixture of twigs and crushed lignite, soaked with rainwater containing a decomposition accelerator. After the last farewell, the fully certified humusaters pour more of the solution over the body of the deceased. They then shape the pile to make it a kind of "living monument," which they cover with a layer of straw, crushed dead leaves, possibly mixed with dried grass clippings. This blanket is necessary to keep the body warm. You see, all this is both natural and yes ... humane!*

— *But what about the chimneys?*

— *For Returnees without family, there is no need to reserve a place. They go in the central structure, which is actually a large humusater. The chimneys are simply used to remove smoke, as composting organic material releases heat.*

— *So, this garden—this forest behind the chimneys—is actually a gigantic ... graveyard?*

— *That word is no longer really in use, you know. This is the most harmonious action possible. Why ruin it by bringing up that sad, outdated image? This is the garden of life in its noblest sense, that of the fusion of the animal with its Mother!*

— *What happens after that?*

— *After three months decomposition, the "monument" has shrunk right down, as the flesh has already been digested by all the soil micro-organisms and bacteria and transformed into soil. So, the humusaters remove the metal prostheses and non-biodegradable materials to prevent soil pollution. The bones are all clean now and they powder them to release the calcium and phosphorous. Then, they rebuild the "monument" by gently mixing what's left with some clay pellets and certain biodynamic preparations, adjust the moisture content, and it's good to go again. Until finally, the proteins of the flesh are chemically associated with the natural polymers of the plant cellulose and you have soil.*

— *Is this the end of the process?*

— *The best is yet to come! At the end of the process, we have the "super-compost," which the experienced humusaters use to regenerate the land most abused by human exploitation: arable land, industrial wasteland, dredging soil ... to plant trees that will permanently fix some of the excess CO_2 responsible for climate change ... What you called "euthanasia" is, in reality, the gift of life.*

— *I understand.*

— *Yes, now you understand. What you have here is not an abattoir, but the most beautiful accomplishment of Man, the ultimate expression of his reconciliation with the All Living.*[131]

---

131 The description of the Forest Garden of Metamorphosis, including certain choice expressions with which it is graced, is borrowed from humusation.org, website of the Belgian public utility foundation "Metamorphosis, Dying then creating Life," which advocates the legalization of humusation. This is not fiction.

Main Conclusions of this Work
(...for those in a hurry)

*To limit the spheres where freedom of choice can be
exercised is to undermine the very essence of man.*

Isaiah Berlin [132]

1. Environmentalism is not a sub-branch of Marxism;

2. Malthusian predictions on the theme of resource depletion for
the past 250 years—by Malthus, Jevons, Ehrlich, Meadows,
etc.—have all been proven wrong, without exception;

3. Environmentalist ethic is "physisist" and de-anthropocentric:
environmentalists wholeheartedly favor nature without discrim-
ination; Man suffers an ontological degradation unprecedented
in western tradition;

4. If human CO_2 is the problem, then Man is the problem (totalizing environmentalist analytic);

5. If human CO_2 is the problem, then Man must be restricted, constrained, and governed in all his activities (totalitarian environmentalist algorithm);

132 Isaiah Berlin, *Liberty* {extract translated from French version: *Eloge de la liberté*,
Paris, Calmann-Lévy, 1990 (1969), p.48}

6. The abolition of individual freedom does not "derive" from the totalitarian environmentalist algorithm: it *is* the algorithm;

7. The humanicidal tendency of environmentalism is consistent with its postulates;

8. The de-population of the Earth is the final solution[133] to the environmental problem;

9. As a science, ecology should not seek to enter the political arena; when it ventures into it, it ceases to be a science;

10. Environmentalism is totalitarianism.

Each of these propositions is structurally refutable. Propositions 3 to 8 have been fully adopted by a significant number of environmentalist intellectuals.

Power is in inflicting pain and humiliation. Power is in tearing human minds to pieces and putting them together again in new shapes of your own choosing. Do you begin to see, then, what kind of world we are creating? It is the exact opposite of the stupid hedonistic Utopias that the old reformers imagined. A world of fear and treachery is torment, a world of trampling and being trampled upon, a world which will grow not less but MORE merciless as it refines itself. Progress in our world will be progress towards more pain. The old civilizations claimed that they

---

133 "Final solution"? Isn't using that expression outrageous? Using the term used by the National Socialists to designate the extermination of the Jews?! You don't have to go that far back. Hans Jonas, the foremost thinker of humanophobic environmentalism, speaks specifically of the *"final solution"—die endgültige Lösung—*to the environmental problem in an illuminating interview with *Der Spiegel*, 1992: https://www.spiegel.de/spiegel/print/d-13680535.html Cfr. Annex 2 of this work.

were founded on love or justice. Ours is founded upon hatred. In our world, there will be no emotions except fear, rage, triumph, and self-abasement. Everything else we shall destroy – everything. Already we are breaking down the habits of thought, which have survived from before the Revolution. We have cut the links between child and parent, and between man and man, and between man and woman.

George Orwell (1984)

Alternative Afterword

The material conditions of life will continue to get better for most people, in most countries, most of the time, indefinitely.[134]

Julian Simon, "The Doomslayer," *Wired*, January 1, 1997

Now, at the end of this work, you are probably asking yourself the question: even if it is all true, so what if Man actually warms the planet by emitting CO_2?

Are we, therefore, condemned to submit ourselves to the totalitarian algorithm of environmentalism, if only to survive?

Allow me, in all modesty, to attempt to answer these questions.

Let us first point out that around the world tens of thousands of scientists—that is practitioners of 'hard' science—have radically divergent opinions from the IPCC's "scientific" work.[135]

---

134 "The material conditions of life will continue to get better for most people, in most countries, most of the time, *indefinitely*. Within a century or two, all nations and most of humanity will be at or above today's Western living standards... I also speculate, however, that many people will continue to *think and say* that the conditions of life are getting *worse*." (italics added) https://www.wired.com/1997/02/the-doomslayer-2/

135 The Oregon Petition (http://www.oism.org/pproject/), The Heidelberg Appeal (https://americanpolicy.org/2002/03/29/the-heidelberg-appeal/), The Leipzig Declaration (https://journals.sagepub.com/doi/abs/10.1260/0958305042886732?journalCode=e-aea), The Manhattan Declaration (http://www.climatescienceinternational.org/index.php?Itemid=54) etc.

Let us remember that CO_2 is not a pollutant, let alone a poison, that there is no life without CO_2, and that we exhale CO_2 every time we breathe.

It should be noted that the US government was recently planning to set up a scientific commission charged with reviewing the IPCC's literature.[136]

Let us also note, that many scientists argue that the climate has always evolved and that even though Man could play a marginal role in the slight warming currently observed—which no one is disputing—it is, by no means, problematic in itself.

Let us conclude by emphatically emphasizing that it is utterly ludicrous to claim that the work of the IPCC is scientific, that the SR15—the last special report of the IPCC—is anything other than a grotesque shambles, whose scientific value is non-existent for the methodological reasons mentioned.

Like communism and Nazism, in the long term, environmentalism cannot triumph, for it presupposes an integral reprogramming of human Nature to that of a small, submissive creature indistinguishable from a lapdog or a rabbit in headlights.

Man! Isn't he better than that? Isn't he something better, something other than an introspective mammal? The tremendous progress that has led us to grow and improve the conditions of life on our planet will lead us to spread life across the solar system, and beyond.

This is the glorious destiny of humanity; on these grounds Man deserves our respect, our trust, and our love.

---

136 Alex Newman, "Massive Coalition Backs Trump's Climate Science Committee," *New American*, 20 March 2019, https://www.thenewamerican.com/tech/environment/item/31791-massive-coalition-backs-trump-s-climate-science-committee

Annex 1—The Latest IPCC Report (SR15)

This is the first time in the history of mankind that we are setting ourselves the task of intentionally, within a defined period of time, changing the economic development model that has been reigning for at least 150 years, since the Industrial Revolution.

Christiana Figueres, Executive Secretary of the United Nations Framework Convention on Climate Change (UFCCC), 2015[137]

In its latest special report "Global warming of 1.5°C" (SR15), the IPCC proposes four scenarios to allow the Earth to cap global warming at 1.5°C.

A full appreciation of all four scenarios can be gained by the close reading of SR15. One key point that all four scenarios hold in common is that CO_2 emissions are reduced to virtually nothing by 2050.

The four scenarios implement, to varying degrees, so-called Carbon Dioxide Removal (CDR) techniques, which compensate for human CO_2 emissions:

---

137 https://www.unric.org/en/latest-un-buzz/29623-figueres-first-time-the-world-economy-is-transformed-intentionally Madame Figueres seems unaware that the industrial revolution actually began in 1750.

"All pathways that limit global warming to 1.5°C with limited or no overshoot project the use of carbon dioxide removal (CDR) on the order of 100–1000 Gtco2 over the twenty-first century. CDR would be used to compensate for residual emissions and, in most cases, achieve net negative emissions to return global warming to 1.5°C following a peak (high confidence). CDR deployment of several hundreds of Gtco2 is subject to multiple feasibility and sustainability constraints (high confidence). Significant near-term emissions reductions and measures to lower energy and land demand can limit CDR deployment to a few hundred Gtco2 without reliance on bioenergy with carbon capture and storage (BECCS)" (p.19).

The IPCC defines these CDR techniques as follows:

"Carbon dioxide removal (CDR): anthropogenic activities removing CO_2 from the atmosphere and durably storing it in geological, terrestrial, or ocean reservoirs, or in products. It includes existing and potential anthropogenic enhancement of biological or geochemical sinks and direct air capture and storage but excludes natural CO_2 uptake not directly caused by human activities" (p.26).[138]

The only likely scenario mentioned—read as the only one that is in any way realistic—is the fourth, that of a continuation not only of CO_2 emissions, but of their *growth*. Countries such as China and India have lifted hundreds of millions of citizens out of poverty by developing economically and, thus, by consuming more energy; they will persist in this direction and nothing will deter them—certainly not the "Paris Agreement"—which expressly allows them to continue increasing their CO_2 emissions for years to come.

---

138 CDR is discussed up to p.118 and chapter 4 of the report.

Logically, it is this fourth scenario that foresees the most intensive use of CDR techniques: "Emissions reductions are mainly achieved through technological means, making strong use of CDR."

The problem is that these CDR techniques—also known as CCS, Carbon Capture and Storage, and CCU for Carbon Capture and Utilization[139]—are meaningless from both an economic and an energy perspective. They consume between 10% and 100% (*sic*) of the energy produced. The European Commission has tried to promote these techniques, but all projects were abandoned.[140] As the IPCC acknowledges in the report, "Most CDR technologies remain largely unproven to date."[141]

The fourth scenario is, therefore, equally implausible.

The other three scenarios presuppose a reduction in energy consumption, which would be the miraculous result of "economic convergence and international cooperation, as well as shifts towards sustainable and healthy consumption pattern" (Scenario 2) and ... technological progress.

Another major feature of this report is its enthusiasm for future technological progress. All four scenarios assume tremendous technological advances.

The difficulty is that technological advance and economic growth are consubstantial.

---

139 The second envisions storing CO_2 for reutilization, the first envisions storing it permanently.

140 I thank Prof. Samuel Furfari for his insight into these technical issues.

141 SR15, p.121, p.158 and Chapter 4; see, in particular, page 394 : " there are uncertainties about how much it would cost to deploy (...) a CDR technique, given that removing CO_2 from the air requires considerable energy." (*sic*)

The first scenario predicts a collapse in energy consumption "while living standards rise.".. through the application of alchemy, and not reason, one assumes.

Finally, starting from page 20 (of 32), the SR15 decision makers' summary[142] attempts to explain that the implementation of these different scenarios will, at the same time, allow an "eradication of poverty."

An IPCC report is nothing but a reprint of the Meadows Report, except it's in color.

Since it is based entirely on *hypothetical* technological advances, the SR15 is essentially non-refutable, in the sense that Popper gives the term, therefore, it is entirely outside the field of science.

It is not surprising that such fanciful documents are published; they will be published as long as the IPCC is funded by the tax-payer, who has no choice in the matter, anyway. Amazingly, nearly half a century after the Meadows Report, such nonsense still finds an audience.

In short, the report lacks a fifth scenario: the continuation of eco-nomic growth, poverty reduction, and worldwide growth in CO_2 emissions, regardless of whether Europe continues on its chosen path to servitude or not.

Which of these five scenarios would you bet your money on?

142 See chapter 5 of the report.

Appendix 2—Hans Jonas, non-thinker

I loved Marx once. His inspiration, his vigor, his originality, his consistency, his style, his intransigence in sticking to principles that were not without reason, and his formidable productivity.

I admire Keynes, his ability to collate the economic material of his day in a systematic and radically original conceptual structure.

However, I do not recognize in any way the value that these two authors so cherished: substantive equality. Real equality seems, to me, counternatural, impossible to achieve or conceptualize, and horribly harmful in its actual effect.

I do not love Hans Jonas; I have no admiration for him, and I can barely fend off a feeling of contempt.

In seeking to better Cartesian dualism—which recognizes the human soul as a reality distinct from matter—Jonas offers no alternative nor regress towards a kind of Spinozism by default. Jonas simply postulates the supernatural, "an emanation of matter that has managed to become aware of itself and feels."[143] This hocus-pocus has no rational basis but must stem from a form of naive animism pre-dating civilization.

When Jonah suggests replacing humanist anthropology—Man the epicenter of all things, anthropocentric   with a "metaphysic of Nature,"[144] he does not seem to be aware that the expression "metaphysic of Nature" is a contradiction *in terminis*; by definition, what is metaphysical is that beyond Nature. If we are limited

---

143 *Esprit, op. cit., p.16.*

144 *Ibidem.*

to the natural or physical world, there is no more anthropology; there is no more metaphysic; there is literally nothing *rational* anymore, as Jonas, a pupil of Heidegger, should not fail to know.

Finally, when Jonas speaks of a final solution[145] to the ecological problem, we cannot ignore—as we could not allow it to pass without mention before—the terrible connotations of the term "final solution." A Jewish German himself, Jonas fled Nazi Germany.

What a pity that Mr. Jonas did not confine himself to his first field: the study of Gnostic authors, at which he was not *too* bad.

145 *Der Spiegel, op. cit.*, 1992.

Acknowledgements

I would like to thank Prof. Ernest Mund and Prof. Samuel Furfari for their critique and suggestions and Dr Pierre Debatty for his critical re-reading and the numerous invaluable sources that he provided. I must also thank Henri Lepage, Nicolas De Pape, and Thomas Godefridi for their critical comments and finally Andrew McDonald. It goes without saying that I, alone, am accountable for the conclusions of this work.

Printed in Great Britain
by Amazon